## "Made up you... about the jo...

Ricco's arm moved along the bench as he asked.

Vicky flushed as his hand brushed her neck. "Look, Mr. Salvatore, let's get something straight. I might be interested in a job with your firm, but on my own merits. I don't want you making a job for me with the idea that I might be available for more private duties outside working hours!"

"I could lose my temper with you, Miss Lloyd," he snapped, suddenly grim-faced. "Do you really think I need to go to such lengths to get a woman? Or do you merely think you're so ultradesirable that every man you meet is going to crumble?"

Oh, not again, Vicky thought, getting up to walk away. Like it or not, every time they met, something certainly did happen—between them and inside herself!

**CHARLOTTE LAMB** began to write "because it was one job I could do without having to leave the children." Now writing is her profession. She has had more than forty Harlequin novels published since 1978. "I love to write," she explains, "and it comes very easily to me." She and her family live in a beautiful old home on the Isle of Man, between England and Ireland. Charlotte spends eight hours a day working at her typewriter—and she enjoys every minute of it.

## Books by Charlotte Lamb

A VIOLATION
SECRETS

### HARLEQUIN PRESENTS
842—WHO'S BEEN SLEEPING IN MY BED?
851—SLEEPING DESIRE
874—THE BRIDE SAID NO
898—EXPLOSIVE MEETING

### HARLEQUIN ROMANCE
2696—KINGFISHER MORNING
2804—THE HERON QUEST

# CHARLOTTE LAMB

## heat of the night

**Harlequin Books**

TORONTO • NEW YORK • LONDON
AMSTERDAM • PARIS • SYDNEY • HAMBURG
STOCKHOLM • ATHENS • TOKYO • MILAN

Harlequin Presents first edition April 1987
ISBN 0-373-10971-7

Original hardcover edition published in 1986
by Mills & Boon Limited

# CHAPTER ONE

SUSAN met her at Pisa airport, as they had arranged on the phone the day before, but Vicky could have walked right past her without being recognised. Susan's head didn't even turn, she was staring fixedly at the queues of people emerging through the barrier, and when Vicky touched her arm she jumped about three feet in the air.

'It's me,' Vicky hissed in a low voice, and watched her cousin's jaw drop with a sense of relieved satisfaction. If she could fool Susan she could fool anyone.

'Vicky?' Susan instinctively whispered too, her eyes as big as saucers. 'I don't believe it! What have you done to yourself?'

'Let's get out of here,' said Vicky. 'We can talk once we're sure we can't be overheard.' She headed for the exit with her case and Susan, after a stunned pause, followed.

'My car's just over there.' The airport building was surrounded by car parks which were almost full. Vicky felt the heat of the sun striking through her white wool jacket with faint surprise; she had forgotten that it was likely to be warmer in Italy than it had been in rain-drenched England. She had come away in such a rush that she hadn't done much thinking of any kind; she had merely fled to the only close relative she had in the world, knowing that she could trust Susan implicitly.

'Did you have a good flight? Not too bumpy over
the Alps?' Susan asked as they walked across the
tarmac towards the small red Fiat parked right at
the back of the area. 'The last time we came back
from London I almost last my lunch. It felt as if we
were on the end of a bit of string being swung to and
fro by an excited kid! It isn't usually that bumpy,
but I bet you were glad to see the last of the
mountains.'

'I was a little nervous, looking down on all those
snowy peaks.' She had had too much on her mind,
though, to indulge in flying nerves. Her only real
fear during the flight had been that when she landed
she might find a pushing, yelling mob of camera-
men and reporters waiting for her. Compared to
that nightmare, flying over the Alps had been a
piece of cake. 'How's David?' she asked, and her
cousin turned a smiling face towards her.

'Oh, fine. He loves working here. He gets on very
well with his boss, and the countryside around
Florence is so beautiful, every weekend we get out
to discover new villages, marvellous scenery, have
lunch under the trees in some open-air café. David's
all for the culture bit, of course, you know how keen
he is on Italian art, and heaven knows he can drown
in the stuff round here. We still haven't even
brushed the surface in Florence itself, but once the
warm weather starts you can't move there for
tourists, so we've concentrated on churches and the
Tuscan hill towns.'

She had unlocked her car and lifted Vicky's case
into the small boot as she talked—talked rather
more than Susan usually did, and Vicky knew her
well enough to guess why. Susan was curious and

puzzled and worried, and tried to cover all three emotions by chattering away.

Susan was slim and pretty, with curly auburn hair and gentle brown eyes. Her colouring and nicely proportioned figure would have made her striking if she had been a little more assured, but even two years of marriage to the man she loved deeply had not lent her any more self-confidence—perhaps it never would. Susan's opinion of herself had been formed at too early an age by an overbearing, sarcastic and contemptuous father. However hard she tried, Susan had never been able to match up to Uncle George's standards; and it had left an indelible mark on her.

Vicky was leaning on the top of the car looking round her curiously. 'How far is it to Florence?'

'I forget exactly how many miles it is, but it takes me just under an hour. I set off at ... oh, dear!' Susan, about to get into her seat, had stiffened, and Vicky felt her nerves prickle as she looked round to see who had put that look into her cousin's face. For a second she was afraid she would see the hounds of the press bearing down on her, baying for blood, but then she realised that Susan was giving a polite, uneasy smile, greeting a man who had just parked his car nearby.

'Hallo, Ricco.' Susan had flushed guiltily, almost as though it was she who was in hiding.

'*Ciao*, Susan.' The voice was deep and caressing, a voice with the sun in it. Vicky felt her cousin's agitation deepen and was curious—what was making Susan so uptight? She had assumed that Susan was nervous on her behalf, but it was far more than that—it was this man who was the root of

her cousin's unease. Vicky studied him thoughtfully, secure behind her sunglasses. Their smoky lenses
hid her eyes from him, which didn't stop him from
staring back as if trying to probe through the dark
glass.

'I'm here to meet someone off the London
plane—is it in yet, do you know?' He sauntered over
to the Fiat, his dark blue eyes making lazy forays
over Vicky's figure in the white jacket and candy-
pink pants, with which she wore a matching top
under the jacket. The outfit was perfect for
travelling in; practically uncreasable and machine
washable, it was both light and cool once she shed
the jacket, as she had done on the plane.

'Yes, most of the passengers have left, so you'd
better hurry,' Susan told him.

He glanced at her and then at Vicky. 'Aren't you
going to introduce us?'

Susan floundered, her eyes appealing to her
cousin. 'Yes, I . . . this is . . .'

Vicky rescued her calmly. 'I'm Ann Lloyd, an old
school friend of Susan's.'

She heard Susan give a muffled sigh of relief—
they had forgotten to think of a false identity for
her, but then this trip had been arranged in such a
hurry there had been no time for lengthy explana-
tions or discussions. She had just asked if she could
come and Susan had said yes, of course, where else
would you go?

'I'm Riccardo Salvatore, one of Susan and
David's neighbours.' He offered his hand and she
rather reluctantly took it. His skin was smooth and
cool, the tanned hand firmly shaped and elegant
with long, sensitive fingers, which clasped hers for a

moment longer than she liked. His accent was only faintly Italian and his English extraordinarily good, a great deal better than her own Italian, but she hadn't needed to know his name to guess his nationality. He was distinctly Latin, a black-haired, long-limbed man of Mediterranean appearance, bronzed and lithe, with strikingly austere features and a mouth which contradicted them. Wide and strongly moulded, it held a mixture of sensuality, humour and cynicism which was at odds with his pared cheekbones, firm jaw and long, arrogant nose.

'Staying long?' he asked, and she shrugged, very conscious of his gaze on her short blonde hair, and hoping he wasn't noticing that it was not her natural colour. She wasn't used to being blonde herself, yet; when she looked into the mirror in the plane's loo she had done a double take for a second, confused and blinking, until she remembered that she had had her hair dyed. She had often wondered what it felt like to be a blonde, but so far she hadn't noticed much difference. Perhaps it was only casual interest that made Riccardo Salvatore stare like that? All the same, he looked as if not much escaped him. She must try not to see him again. How close a neighbour was he? It was clear that he knew Susan well, yet she had hardly been overjoyed to see him.

'Is this your first visit to Florence?'

'Yes.' It would be wisest to keep her replies short and succinct. That way she was less likely to make a slip-up.

'Then you have a unique opportunity ahead of you—I often wish I had new eyes to see my city with. I've lived here most of my life and know it too well. You must let me show you some of my favourite places.'

She smiled coolly, the delicately shaped mouth beneath the dark glasses curving very slightly without real warmth. 'How kind, but Susan has promised to give me a guided tour while I'm here.'

His eyes narrowed as he studied her, very cool, very English, with her smooth clear skin and fair hair that was shaped inwards to her long, slim neck. Vicky caught a glint of derisive impatience in his stare, but before he could say whatever was on the tip of his tongue someone called his name behind them.

'Ricco! Ricco, *caro, c'è qualcosa che . . .*'

They all turned to stare at the woman hurrying towards them on the most amazingly high heels, her slender body swaying in a way that held the eyes of her porter riveted as he followed behind her with what appeared to be enough luggage for a whole party of tourists on a trolley. As the woman came she talked in a melodic, fluid Italian of which Vicky understood about one word in a dozen. It was hard to tell whether she was furious, excited or rapturous to see Riccardo Salvatore, but whichever it was the lady felt it with every fibre. Her husky voice swooped and soared, she gesticulated with her hands, her black eyes flashed, and Riccardo Salvatore listened, smiling. She appeared to amuse him, and at last he interrupted her with a flow of Italian of his own.

The porter leaned on his trolley, enjoying the discussion. Once or twice he intervened to add a comment of his own. Both parties turned on him, and he threw up his hands, shrugging.

*'Va bene, va bene, mi scusi!'*

'Bianca, I want you to meet someone—now, calm down, I'm sorry I wasn't there to meet you, but I met a neighbour.' He murmured introductions as his lady friend turned her sultry eyes on Vicky and Susan. 'This is Bianca Fancelli.'

Susan shyly offered her hand and Bianca languidly brushed her fingers over it. *'Ciao.'* She was beautiful and she knew it, full-breasted, golden-skinned, with a cloud of curling black hair and hips that moved with molten grace. Her lower lip pouted as she gave Susan a reluctant glance and then turned to give Ricco an accusing stare.

*'Che ora è? Non mi sento bene . . .'*

*'Va bene*, Bianca. We'll be on our way in a moment.'

*'Partirò domani!'* she shrieked at him, tossing back her head, and that, at least, Vicky understood. The lady was threatening to leave tomorrow; she was very displeased. Riccardo Salvatore had offended her, he had hung around out in the car park chatting up other women when he should have been in the terminal, dancing attendance on Bianca.

Ricco seemed unperturbed. In fact, he smiled with deep amusement and said to Susan and Vicky, 'She's a singer, and if she keeps screaming like that she's going to ruin her voice; she has a very delicate throat and ought to have more sense.'

'Oh dear,' said Susan, bemused, quite unaware that he was actually talking to Bianca, who understood every word, but whose only response was to make a sound deep in her throat, something between a spitting noise and the snarl of a furious cat.

'Singers!' Ricco sighed. 'Crazy people.'

Vicky had had enough of this particular little soap opera. 'Shall we go?' she asked Susan, opening the passenger door of the Fiat and sliding into her seat. Susan, more politely, said, 'We really should be going . . . nice to see you, Ricco, Miss Fancelli.'

Ricco opened her door for her, put a hand under her elbow to assist her into her seat, threw a brief glance across her at Vicky and smiled mockingly. *'Ciao, a presto!'*

Her face remained cool and his mouth twisted. *'Parla italiano?'*

She shook her head. 'Sorry, I'm afraid not.'

'Then it's time you learnt,' he informed her. 'I'll be happy to give you a few lessons while I'm showing you round Florence.' Before she could snap back that he wasn't teaching her anything or showing her around anywhere, he had closed the door firmly and stood back.

'What does he want, a harem?' growled Vicky as they drove out of the car park. 'I'd have thought his hands were full with the demanding Miss Fancelli, he didn't have to flirt with me.'

'He flirts with everyone.' Susan's eyes were on the road, but her tone held an odd quiver and Vicky watched her, frowning.

'With you, too?' she asked lightly, and heard the involuntary, half-stifled sigh her cousin gave.

'Oh, well . . . yes . . . I'd just laugh if only . . .'

'If only what?' Vicky had known her since they were both in their prams; they had grown up together, living in the same small village five minutes' walk from each other's houses. She could always tell when Susan had something on her mind, and she sensed now that the something currently weighing heavily with her cousin was a six-foot-tall Italian called Riccardo Salvatore. It didn't enter Vicky's head for an instant that Susan might be in love with him. She had seen her cousin's face light up when she talked about her husband. Susan was still passionately in love with David, so what was bothering her? Was Riccardo Salvatore being rather too pressing? Had he been trying to seduce Susan? Vicky remembered the sensual, cynical curve of his mouth, the mocking blue eyes, and could easily imagine it. Susan's blushes, shyness, obvious uneasiness might have given him the idea that she fancied him, was giving him a green light. Ricco Salvatore might be sophisticated; Susan wasn't.

Vicky kept her eyes on her cousin's averted profile. 'Oh, nothing,' Susan said, very pink. 'By the way, this is a Roman road, the old road from Pisa to Florence. We'll be turning on to the autostrada in a minute. We should arrive by three-thirty. That will give you plenty of time to see the villa, have a bath and a rest on your bed if you like before David gets home. He's promised to take us out to dinner tonight if you aren't too tired.' Susan turned a brighter face to her, smiling. 'I hope you aren't! We haven't been out to dinner for ages. I'm looking forward to it.'

Vicky laughed. 'Oh, I'll manage to stagger out. I've been dieting but I don't see why I shouldn't gorge myself on some delicious Italian food once in a while.' Her eyes wandered over the flat landscape, dotted with little houses and vineyards and orchards, half veiled at the moment in a gentle, misty light. Spring was touching the trees with green, the first new leaves. Their colour seemed to run through the valley like green smoke, indefinite, drifting, hard to pin down. Vicky's eyes lifted to the skyline, where a range of hills rose, blue and hazy.

'Those are the Carrara mountains, where the marble comes from, you know? All the sculptors used Carrara marble, they still do if they can afford it, but it's very expensive now. David is going to drag you around to see everything Michelangelo did, so I hope you like sculpture.'

'I'm not in love with it,' Vicky said drily. 'A little culture goes a long way with me, you know that.'

Susan turned to grin at her. 'Well, I told David you used to have to be dragged round art galleries kicking and screaming, but he loves to spread the gospel. That only whetted his appetite. He thinks he'll convert you.'

'Optimist!'

They slowed as they approached the toll which marked the beginning of the autostrada. As they passed through the barrier Vicky leaned back in her seat, watching the other cars. One roared past, sounding its horn. She started, just catching a glimpse of Ricco Salvatore at the wheel of the gleaming red Lamborghini which was already heading away from them at a speed that Susan's little Fiat could not possibly match.

'Aren't you going to tell me what went wrong?' Susan asked quietly a moment later, and Vicky gave a long sigh.

'I had to get away, I couldn't take it any more,' she said after a pause. 'You have no idea what it was like, Susan—a nightmare! Yesterday I woke up, and I knew I had to get away, end it. It was the only way—a sharp break. But if anyone had known what was in my mind there would have been all hell to pay, and I simply couldn't face that, more press, more questions, more photographers and . . .' She stopped talking, her voice harsh. 'So I rang you, and then I booked my flight and kept my fingers crossed that nobody at Heathrow would recognise the name, that there wouldn't be any press around watching people board. You've no idea how much I sweated until I was on the plane and we were taking off!'

Susan took one hand off the wheel and touched her lightly. 'Poor Vicky, I must say I don't think I could have faced it either. Not my scene—all that publicity, being in the limelight all the time. But what about Miller? He must have been shattered when you told him.'

Vicky stiffened in her seat, her eyes on the silver birches and tall, dark cypresses on the slopes above the road. She didn't say anything, and Susan looked round at her, face appalled.

'Vicky! You did tell him! You didn't just go?'

'I wrote to him; posted it on my way to Heathrow.' Vicky felt guilty about doing it that way, but she hadn't dared risk talking to Miller beforehand. Any hint that she meant to run would have been disastrous; he wouldn't have understood and he would have tried to talk her out of it, but far more than that, he would have told Sunny, he told Sunny everything and Sunny, of course, would have picked up a phone and told the press. No, she could'nt have told Miller until she was safely out of the country.

Susan was staring at her with dismay and reproach. 'Oh, Vicky! Poor Miller, what a dreadful shock it will be when he reads your letter, he's going to be so hurt. Don't you think you should have told him to his face? At least talked it over with him! Just going away . . . it doesn't seem very kind.'

Vicky's face was pale and set. She had known how Susan would react; she understood Susan's feelings, and looking at the situation from the outside it was the way most people would react, but then only someone who had been through what she had been through for the last month would understand why she was running away like this.

'Please, Susan, can we change the subject? I had to do it that way and I don't want to talk about it. For the moment, I just want to forget the whole thing.' She sat up straight, her hands locked in her lap. They were very cold, although the sun was warm on her face. 'What are those trees along the centre of the road?' she asked.

'Oleanders,' Susan, said absently, giving them a quick glance. 'In high summer they're covered with the most gorgeous flowers, pink and red. It's quite a sight.' She slowed pace, the car doing a steady forty miles an hour. 'Vicky, didn't you love him?'

Vicky kept her eyes fixed on the passing landscape. Ignoring the question, she asked, 'Is that another airport? I thought Pisa was the nearest one to Florence?'

'It isn't a civil airport, that's a military base. Oh, look, that plane is dropping parachutists!'

As they watched, the sky suddenly filled with delicate, frilly-edged white flowers which floated downwards like petals on a warm wind. The dark doll-like figures hanging beneath the flowers gradually came into view as men in camouflage uniform, but by the time the car had done another few hundred yards the parachutists were out of sight behind some airport buildings.

'I've often thought I'd like to do some parachuting,' Vicky said reflectively. 'I'd like to learn to fly, too. It must give you a great kick, being up there all by yourself.'

Susan didn't seem to agree, her brow was furrowed. 'David's bound to want to know what's going on, Vicky—what am I to tell him?'

'What I just told you.' Vicky glanced at her, biting her lower lip. She hadn't considered how David might react. 'Look, if you think he might disapprove, might not want me around . . .'

'Oh, don't be silly! David likes you, and he's often said we ought to have you to stay with us some time. You're very welcome, you know that. It's just that . . .'

Susan was always starting sentences she didn't finish, a habit which had begun in childhood when she found it so hard to talk to her father. Until quite recently she had stammered whenever she was nervous. Perhaps she still did? Uncle George had a lot to answer for; yet when he died Susan and her mother had cried their eyes out and been in a state of grief for ages afterwards. Even now Aunt Lucy hadn't remarried; the last time Vicky saw her, her aunt had several times mentioned her dead husband, although he had died four years ago.

'Just that what?' probed Vicky, patiently, used to Susan's incoherent way of blurting out confidences.

'Well, he was just joking, Vicky, but he said he

hoped that having you here wouldn't mean that we'd have the *paparazzi* descending on us, too.' Susan gave a nervous, placatory laugh. 'But he was only joking. It's just that Signor Rossi might not like any sort of publicity, David being caught up in any sort of publicity, I mean.'

'Who is Signor Rossi?'

'His boss,' Susan said, sounding astonished that Vicky hadn't known that. 'He's a very kind man, he's always sending us things—fruit, game, that sort of thing. He has a large estate in the hills somewhere, right out in the country. He's very rich.'

'Obviously. And he doesn't like publicity?'

'Well, for the firm, he does, but . . .'

'Not for David? Not the sort of publicity I'd attract, anyway.' Vicky could see the man's point. She didn't like the sort of publicity she had been getting lately, either.

David Bruce had taken up a job in Italy just after his marriage. Until then he had worked for a large multi-national oil company. He was a brilliant engineer, and had gone straight from college to work on oil rigs in the North Sea, but now he was confined to a desk in an office in Florence, having become a white-collar engineer. He was highly paid and had had promotion since joining the Anglo-Italian firm he worked for, but from Susan's letters Vicky had sensed that he had a lingering regret for the days when he worked in the field, getting himself dirty, taking risks, living a more exciting life than he did now when he was just a consultant.

'You did tell David not to mention that I was coming? To anyone at all?' she asked Susan, who nodded.

'Then there's no reason why anyone should ever find out,' said Vicky, staring out of the window as they climbed a tree-shaded hill. 'How much further is it to Florence?'

'You'll see it any minute now; it's just in front of us.'

They cruised along the narrow, winding road and emerged on to an open plateau, and there Vicky caught her first glimpse of Florence. The city was veiled in mist through which floated domes and spires, the warm yellow walls glowing softly in that diffused light, their colours so natural that they looked as if they had grown up from the earth they stood on rather than having been built by the hand of man. They clustered so close together that you could not see the streets.

Vicky leaned forward, mouth parted on a breath of enchantment. 'All the houses seem to be the same colour.' The yellow plaster was close to the colour of pale mustard, and the wavy ancient tiles on the roofs were all rose-red terracotta.

'They call that colour sienna, it means earth,' said Susan, parking the car close to a stone balustrade round a vast square which had been built above the city, looking through the trees, shrubs and flowers of a terraced garden tumbling down into the city itself.

'And that's the Uffizi—down there near the Arno. We'll take you there one day this week. That's where you'll see what David calls *le monstre sacré* of Italian art—Botticelli! If you can get near the paintings, that is—there's usually a crowd six deep round them all. Do you want to get out and take a closer look now, or are you tired? David did say he'd be home early to welcome you to Florence.'

Vicky would have liked to get out and stand there for a long time, gazing down on the city, but she picked up the reluctant note in Susan's voice and knew her cousin wanted to get back home, so she shook her head.

'I can see I'm going to have a strenuous visit, tramping around Florence from art gallery to art gallery, so I'd better conserve my energy for the moment. Anyway, I'm dying to see your little villa.'

Susan laughed, starting the car again, and drove on. 'I'm afraid it is little—we only have two bedrooms and a sitting-room and kitchen. But it's modern. Ricco only had it built two years ago.'

'Ricco?' Vicky was startled.

Susan turned to look at her. 'Yes, didn't you realise that he was our landlord? He lives in an enormous house, it's very old, thirteenth-century. It used to be a convent or monastery or something, but Ricco's family bought it in the seventeenth century and they've lived there ever since. They were in banking.' Susan laughed. 'Banking practically began in Florence, you know, it's the biggest local trade.'

'He's a banker?' Vicky was incredulous, and Susan laughed again.

'Ricco? No, of course not, although that's where all his family money came from—anyway, he had a lot of land with his house, and he wasn't using it, so he built two small villas at the far end of the gardens, and we live in one.'

She slowed to turn into a driveway through a pair of high ironwork gates. Stone lions sat primly, paws together, on top of two tall stone pillars; Vicky just caught sight of them as the car swept past, between rows of cypress trees. 'This is it,' said Susan. 'The Villa Giglio—that means lily, by the way, nothing to do with the famous singer. That's what I thought when we first came.'

'Is that the name of your villa, or of Ricco's?'

'Oh, his—our place is called Villa l'Arancia.'

'Which means?'

'House of the orange tree, or actually trees— there's a little cluster of them but the winter was pretty hard on them, we don't know if they survived it yet.' Susan turned right as she emerged from the rows of cypress. 'If you're quick you can just see Ricco's house through the trees there.'

She slowed, and Vicky peered through drooping branches, seeing sunlight on smooth, warm columns supporting a loggia on the upper floor of a long, two-storey building with the same terracotta tiles and sienna walls that she had seen a few minutes ago in Florence. The brief glimpse was enough to make her realise how old the house must be; it had a shabby beauty in the sunlight, yet even at this distance she could see the flaking paint on woodwork, the cracks in the plaster, the air of decay the whole place wore, even if it wore it with grace and charm.

'Did you say thirteenth-century?'

'That's the legend. It has a maze of rooms, some of them tiny—they look just like the cells of a monastery, very bare and austere. Ricco keeps them whitewashed and mostly empty. He sometimes talks of turning the place into a hotel, but he never gets around to it.'

'He must be rich, having all this land and that

enormous house.'

'I suppose he must,' Susan said uncertainly. 'He never gives the impression of being rich; he wears jeans most of the time, and his clothes are mostly pretty comfortable and shabby.'

'He's rich! They're always keen to look poor. It's people like us, without money, who want to look as if we've got it.'

'Don't be such a cynic!' Susan had threaded her way along another row of cypress and was parking right outside a small, modern, whitewashed villa, of the familiar Mediterranean type you could see everywhere—two-storied, boxlike, built like a dolls' house. This one was given more charm by a pair of small orange trees in high earthenware pots which stood on either side of the front door.

Susan watched her cousin's face as Vicky gazed out at it. 'What do you think?' she asked, anxious for Vicky to like it.

'It's very pretty. Were the orange trees your idea?'

'Ricco's.'

They got out of the car and Susan unlocked the front door while Vicky carried her case. It was obvious at once that the house had been designed for a small family; it was built on the open plan with one area downstairs divided by low half-walls into three separate spaces—a living-room area, a kichen area and a dining area. The walls had been lined with bookshelves and were topped with marble tiles on which stood house plants, giving the place a garden air, spacious, full of light.

'Ricco designed this, too, I suppose?' Vicky was really beginning to dislike him; he seemed omnipresent in her cousin's life.

Susan nodded. 'I think it's terrific, don't you?' She was on the defensive, conscious of Vicky's unspoken reservations.

'Charming,' Vicky agreed, and followed her cousin up the open staircase, built in a warm varnished pinewood, into the smaller of the two bedrooms.

Sunlight flooding in through a wide window showed her a pastel-painted room, one wall fitted with pinewood wardrobes, the décor modern and restrained. A dark blue bowl of some lustrous pottery stood on the window-sill, hyacinths growing in it, giving the air a heady scent.

'It isn't very big, but I think you'll be comfortable,' said Susan, going over to open the window. 'You're our first guest, apart from my mum and David's parents. Mum loves it here, she came for a month last summer. David's mum and dad have only been once, but then we had to cram another bed in here, which didn't leave much space. I'm afraid David's mother was rather disappointed.'

'You still don't get on too well with her?' Vicky was opening her case as she and Susan talked, and together they hung up the dresses and put away lingerie in the thoughtfully designed wardrobes which had a set of drawers built at one side.

Grimacing, Susan shook her head. 'She thought David could have done better for himself than me. She's very ambitious for him.'

'I think David couldn't have done better,' Vicky said firmly, smiling.

Susan went down to make some tea when they had emptied the case, and Vicky had a quick shower and changed into a silky yellow cotton dress with a scooped neckline and tight waist. The skirt swirled around her calves as she walked over to the window to stare at the terracotta roof of Ricco Salvatore's house, which she could just see through the trees. Was he there now, with his excitable lady-friend? Perhaps they were making up their quarrel. Vicky could easily imagine how—Bianca Fancelli had such sultry, inviting eyes, and Vicky didn't see Ricco Salvatore turning their invitation down.

A swallow darted past, a flash of blue and black, the forked tail quivering. She had a brief glimpse of its beak, full of small twigs; it was nest-building, another omen of spring. She followed its flight absently. It vanished under the eaves of Ricco's house, and then she saw that a small colony of swallows had set up residence there in nests of clay and twigs, baked dry by the Italian sun.

Vicky sighed, her shoulders shuddering. Now that she was alone and no one could see her she found it hard to pretend to be cheerful.

By the time she left, she had realised that she was no longer in love with Miller. She had made a mistake; what she had taken for love had been infatuation, yet even now he still had some hold on her. If she let herself think about him she felt a little tremor of response. He and Ricco Salvatore had this much in common—they were both flirts. Had Miller not been an instinctive flirt they would never have met, because they hardly moved in the same worlds, their paths would never have crossed in the normal way.

Vicky had worked in the design department of a small fashion house, her days there long and crammed with work. She lived in a modest flat in a north London borough which still had some pretence of being in the country; trees lined the streets, there was a little river, now too often polluted with industrial waste, and several large parks. All the houses had gardens, and in summer it was a pleasant place to live. Vicky had had several boy-friends in the past, but when she met Miller she had been heartfree, perhaps even ready to fall in love, and the way in which they met was so romantic and unexpected that it had pushed her headlong into an affair before she knew what was happening.

She had been walking in Hyde Park, very early one autumn morning, under the burnished trees which had just begun to shed their leaves. She had heard the thud of hoofs behind her on a bridle track running alongside the grass she was walking over and had glanced round, smiling, a fresh wind blowing her brown hair across her face. She had been feeling happy; it was such a lovely morning and her walk had been invigorating. The sight of the tall man riding his gleaming black horse seemed the perfect finishing touch.

What she hadn't expected was that the rider should suddenly veer towards her, putting his mount at the gallop. Vicky stood stock still, mouth open in shock, thinking for one horrified second that he was going to knock her down. She should have run, of course, but it all happened too fast. One moment she was frozen there, staring; the next a long arm scooped her up, her feet left the ground and she was pulled across the saddle in front of the laughing rider, held too tightly to feel scared, cradled against him as he rode on under the trees.

Her heart had been beating like a drum, but she hadn't been frightened, she had started to laugh, and Miller had looked down at her then, laughing too.

That was when she had recognised him, and her jaw had dropped. Miller had seen that dazed expression and realised what it meant. His eyes danced with amusement.

'Yeah, it's me,' he said, as if she had asked a question.

She had seen a huge photograph of him in that morning's paper as she ate her breakfast. She had been working half the night on a rush job for her boss and had slept on a couch in the office, that was why she was up so early, before London was really awake. She had gone out to have breakfast at a small café and bought a morning paper to read while she ate. Miller had been on the front page. His latest film was opening in London that week and he was over from America to publicise it. Vicky had vaguely noticed his lean, dark-skinned features, skimmed over the story under the picture. She wasn't a particular fan of his, although she had seen some of his films and enjoyed them. The news that he was in London hadn't excited her, and she had certainly never imagined in her wildest dreams that she might ever meet him, let alone that he might snatch her up and gallop off with her.

It seemed too much like a scene from one of his films, and after the first disbelieving shock she looked around among the trees. The park was almost empty; a few early morning joggers ran along the paths and a squirrel was frisking up a russet-leaved oak, but otherwise they might have been alone in a wilderness.

'Is this some sort of publicity stunt?' she asked warily as he let his horse slow to a walk, the reins loose in his fingers.

'See any press around?' he had drawled, grinning wickedly.

He had a natural charm, and even if he had not been so good-looking he would probably have been irresistible to her that morning. Although she did not know it then, Miller had been in much the same mood, euphoric and reckless, wide open to what hit them both as they looked into each other's eyes.

Oh, yes, it had been wildly romantic at the start, but it had left her with a sour aftertaste which she was sure would take a long time to wear off.

# CHAPTER TWO

'WHAT about your job? Has your boss given you time off or did you just walk out on him, too?'

'David!' Susan's voice was appalled, but Vicky gave David a dry little smile, accepting the justice of the question.

'I was fired a month ago.'

David stared at her, frowning, but Susan's mouth opened in a gasp of dismay and sympathy.

'Fired? Did the firm get into trouble? You mean you were made redundant?'

'I mean I was fired. My boss had had enough. His patience ran out. He'd had enough of his clients being unable to get into the building through a solid wall of media people, he'd had enough of me vanishing for half the day after Sunny had whisked me off for lunch which turned out to be being eaten in Paris or Madrid or wherever Miller happened to be doing publicity. I think the final straw was when my boss sent me out to buy him a hot dog and I didn't show up again for four hours. When he'd stopped shouting I put on my coat and left. There seemed little point in telling him that Sunny had literally kidnapped me, dragged me into the car in spite of my protests and driven me to Sussex to see Miller sailing his damn yacht!'

They had both listened to her furious, gunfire recital in stupefied silence. Susan got up from the couch where she was sitting beside her husband and ran over to kneel down next to Vicky, hugging her.

'How awful, you poor darling! Why didn't you say it had been that bad?' She turned to eye her husband accusingly. 'Say you're sorry to Vicky, she's been through a tough time.'

'Sorry, Vicky,' David said obediently. He was a large, rugged man a good ten years older than his wife, with rough wiry brown hair and dark eyes, a sallow complexion which had taken the sun far more than Susan's skin had done, and shoulders and a deep chest which rippled with muscles. Vicky had been delighted when her cousin married someone so stable and easy-going. Susan was a vulnerable girl, insecure and uncertain about herself after her difficult childhood. Vicky had believed that David would give her cousin the secure affection she needed, and since the marriage, Susan had certainly blossomed. Her letters had been lively and cheerful and she looked well, but, tanned and healthy though she was, Vicky still sensed that something was wrong between husband and wife. They were far too polite with each other, far too careful. Vicky suspected that they were putting on an act for her benefit.

Looking at his watch, David said he must go and change and then they'd go out to dinner in Florence. Giving Vicky and Susan a placatory smile, he added, 'I've managed to book a table at Pinchiorri's.'

'Pinchiorri's!' Susan sounded taken aback, her eyes widening. 'Can we . . .' She broke off whatever she had been about to say, looking hurriedly at Vicky and forcing a smile. 'Well, that's a lovely idea, David. Vicky, you're in for a treat. Pinchiorri's is the best restaurant in Florence; their menu is supposed to be fabulous, and I've been told that their wine cellar is out of this world—not that we've ever been there yet. I've been dying to eat there, but we couldn't ... well, hadn't you better hurry, David? It's a quarter to seven already.'

'Give me ten minutes,' said David, sprinting to the hall. They heard his feet thudding on the wooden stairs. Susan had got to her feet too. She drifted towards the kitchen with the tea tray.

'You keep talking about Sunny—I'm not sure who he is . . .'

'Miller's agent, or manager, I'm not sure what to call him. He runs Miller's life.' Vicky's voice was cold and hostile. 'And he wanted to run mine.' Her lip curled in distaste at things she had no intention of telling Susan; her cousin would only have been upset if she knew how much of an interest in her Sunny had taken. Susan knew nothing of the sort of world Sunny and Miller inhabited, and she was better off not knowing.

Susan looked up at the ceiling, through which they could hear David wandering around the bedroom above. He was pulling out drawers and slamming cupboards. 'He's looking for his tie and socks,' Susan said. 'I'd better go and help before he starts shouting.'

A moment later, Vicky heard Susan and David talking in the room above. They were obviously trying to keep their voices down, but this little house was not built for privacy; the walls were too thin, the spaces too open. Vicky couldn't pick out their actual words, but one thing was obvious: they were quarrelling.

She frowned. Susan sounded anxious—about what? Vicky had noticed the expression on her cousin's face when David said he had booked a table at Pinchiorri's. It was obviously a very expensive restaurant, and Susan felt David couldn't afford to take them there. Was that what they were arguing about now? Vicky bit down on her lower lip, forehead creased, then picked up her purse and checked that she had the folder of traveller's cheques she had got from the bank the afternoon before she left London. She wasn't going to let David bankrupt himself on her account. She would have to be tactful, choose exactly the right moment, then insist on paying the bill herself.

She had left in such a hurry that she hadn't had time to make arrangements for having money transferred from her bank to Florence, but in a way that might be just as well. Nobody could trace her through her bank; she had taken the precaution of having the cheques made out in dollars, which could be cashed in any country.

She had asked the post office to readdress all her incoming mail to her aunt, Susan's mother, who could then forward it to Florence. Vicky hadn't wanted to leave any loose ends for Sunny to follow.

Above her head, David's voice was raised a few decibels. 'I don't approve of any of this! She should have talked to him, face to face. No, okay, Susan, it isn't my business, but if you ask me this guy is well out of it. Vicky was never a serious type, now was she?'

Vicky swung away and walked to the french windows, suppressing a smile. Absolutely right, David, she thought, staring out at the roses, which were showing tight, tiny green buds. I was never the serious type.

Odd to think of oneself as a type. It lessened the feeling of being an individual, a person, making private decisions about private matters. Types acted all in one way, like computers, didn't they? They were programmed, fed instructions which they must follow. How did you decide which type you were? How did David see himself?

The serious type, she felt, yes, definitely—David would see himself as the serious type. Miller? He had been the glamorous type, no question of that. And Sunny?

She clenched her hands at her side, her mouth twisting with distaste. She didn't even want to consider what type he was—a rogue that had escaped from the factory with half the programming uncompleted. Why did Miller let Sunny run his life? He didn't do a thing until Sunny had given the okay; the man dominated Miller, his actions and thoughts as well as his career. If Vicky hadn't fled, Sunny would have tried to dominate her, too.

That prospect had made Vicky feel very serious indeed.

A few moments later Susan and David came down together, smiling too brightly, like people who have had a row but don't want you to know it. Vicky was sorry for David; he had obviously decided to take her to Pinchiorri's as a gesture of welcome which he couldn't really afford, simply to please his wife, and all he had got for his trouble was a row with Susan over the expense.

As they drove back into Florence down the hill Vicky wondered how much rent they had to pay

Ricco Salvatore. Far more than they could afford, she suspected, but then they hadn't had to furnish the house themselves. Susan had told her that Ricco had picked out all the furniture and was responsible for the upkeep and decoration of the house. His gardener came over once a week to do any heavy work in the garden for Susan, too, although she enjoyed looking after the flowers and shrubs herself.

The restaurant was situated on the ground floor of a fifteenth-century palace right in the heart of the city in the Via Ghibellina, close to the Piazza Santa Croce. David dropped them on the Lungarno, the road running along beside the River Arno, and drove off to find somewhere to park before walking back to join them at the restaurant. Florence was a city being strangled by traffic; the narrow medieval streets were unsuitable for cars, and the area round the Piazza della Signoria, where tourists most tended to cluster to see the Uffizi and the Palazzo Vecchio, had been made a pedestrian precinct, but there were cars everywhere on the streets where Vicky and Susan walked that evening, and parking was obviously impossible.

The air was cooler now; Vicky was glad of the white wool jacket which she had had to discard when she first arrived. Her eyes roamed curiously over the old buildings which they passed in the narrow streets. There were plenty of people about, crowding the pavements, forcing her and Susan to step off into the road at risk to life and limb from passing cars because the pavements were so narrow that two people could not walk abreast, but when they crossed the Piazza Santa Croce there was certainly space enough. It was a vast, open square with the enormous Franciscan church at one side.

'Michelangelo and Galileo are buried there,' Susan told her as she paused to stare at the façade.

'It's hideous,' said Vicky, and Susan laughed.

'Well, it isn't the most beautiful church in the world, but it has some wonderful art in it. David's going to take you there, so beware!'

'Michelangelo probably died of shock after seeing the place for the first time!'

'Oh, it didn't look like this when he was alive. I'm afraid an Englishman is responsible for the façade, as any self-respecting Italian would rush to tell you. The façade was added in the nineteenth century, so was the bell tower.'

'Gothic style—yes, I might have guessed it was Victorian. It's a nice big square, anyway.'

'They used to play football matches in it during the sixteenth century. Much nicer to watch out here than behind barbed wire fences the way they do today, don't you think?'

The sun was setting as they strolled towards the Ciofi-Iacometti palace, the ground floor of which had been turned into a restaurant. Vicky looked up, her eyes dazed by the roseate light running across the sky. Half blind, she walked beside Susan, not seeing where she was going, so that it was Susan who first noticed the man in the pale lightweight suit standing outside the palace entrance.

'Ricco!'

Startled, Vicky stared, seeing his lean face through a dazzle of gold.

'*Ciao*, Susan. Are you eating here tonight, too?' His deep voice was becoming familiar already. Vicky focused on him, her instincts warily picking up her cousin's barely disguised anxiety and Ricco Salvatore's mockery. He was smiling at Susan, but there was an odd glint in his eye. What went on between Susan and this man? Vicky knew there was something between them, something her cousin tried to hide from her, did not want her to guess.

'You're dining here?' Susan's face went pale and then blushed. 'Oh.'

Ricco flicked a look at Vicky, his black lashes touched with gilt in the fading sunlight. He looked very elegant; a tall, lean-hipped man whose clothes had a panache which to Vicky suggested very expensive tailoring.

'Are you alone, you two?' His eyes were skimming over her from her short blonde hair to her feet. 'Did you have a rest this afternoon, Miss Lloyd? Flying can be very tiring. Bed is the best place when you're so tense.' It was polite small talk—but how did he manage to invest it with an undercurrent of other meaning?

'Yes, thank you,' she said, and at the same time Susan stammered, 'No, we aren't alone—I mean, David will be joining us any minute.'

'And Miss Lloyd is playing gooseberry? A threesome is always awkward, isn't it? I'm eating alone, would you mind if I joined you?'

Susan took a gulp of air, pink to her hairline. She couldn't have looked more horrified if Ricco Salvatore had announced that he ate roast mice on toast, but while she floundered trying to think of a polite way of rejecting his suggestion Ricco took matters out of her hand and calmly seized Vicky's elbow, steering her into the building.

'Shall we go in and have an aperitif while we wait

for David?' he murmured.

Vicky threw her cousin a glance, wry and impatient, but there seemed little point in pulling herself out of the grip Ricco had on her arm, so she went with him and Susan unhappily followed them.

'What happened to Miss Fancelli?' Vicky asked as an attentive waiter showed them to a table, smiling as he greeted Ricco by name.

'She went to sleep as soon as she got to her hotel. She's a night bird; she'll wake up and feel hungry around midnight.'

'She isn't staying with you, then?'

He turned cool blue eyes on her. 'No, my house isn't big enough.'

Her brows shot up. 'It looks enormous.' She remembered the long, rambling building which Susan had described as a maze of rooms. What sort of house was Bianca Fancelli used to if Ricco's wasn't big enough for her? Was she very rich, or merely very demanding?

'Oh, it's large,' Ricco agreed drily. 'But if it had a hundred rooms it wouldn't be big enough to hold both myself and Bianca. Having her under the same roof is a little like living in the centre of a maelstrom. All singers have temperament; Bianca simply has twice as much as anyone else, but then her voice is twice as good, so we have to take her as she is. Have you ever heard her sing?'

'I've never heard of her,' Vicky admitted. 'What sort of singer is she?'

His blue eyes were incredulous. 'What sort of . . . my dear Miss Lloyd, I'm speechless! She is a mezzo-soprano, one of the best in the world, in my opinion; certainly one of the best in Italy, and we have a great many first-class mezzos.'

'Oh, opera?'

He regarded her ironically. 'You don't like opera?'

'I didn't say that.' She felt defensive, picking up the dryness of his voice. 'I just don't know much about it. I've seen a few operas, but I'm not particularly musical.'

'Vicky's a fashion designer,' Susan explained with pride, and Ricco's brows lifted.

'Really? A famous one?'

'No,' Vicky said stubbornly, lifting her chin. 'And I'm not the sort of designer Susan implied—I design the fabrics which are used by the man who designs the clothes,' She paused, her eyes regretful. 'I did, anyway.' Until Sunny saw to it that she lost her job!

'You did? Does that mean you've changed your job?'

She shrugged. She didn't want to tell him all the details of her private life. 'Yes.' The crisply succinct answer didn't stop him asking further questions; apparently a slammed door didn't register with Ricco Salvatore.

'So what do you do now?'

'At the moment, nothing. I'm on holiday.'

He studied her, his blue eyes narrow gleaming slits, but as his lips parted, no doubt to deliver yet another question, David loomed up beside their table looking at Ricco like someone discovering a tarantula in his bath.

Susan burst into nervous gabbling. 'Oh, there you are, darling—guess who we met on the doorstep outside here? Ricco was going to eat alone and so . . .' Her voice trailed into miserable silence as David turned his furious eyes on her.

'And so I wondered if you would all be my guests tonight?' Ricco stepped in smoothly with a sunny smile, ignoring David's glower. 'As there are three of you and one of me it seems a very sensible idea. Four's such a comfortable number, and as I've been offering to be Miss Lloyd's guide around Florence I can start right away by telling her about this place. The palace has a fascinating history.'

'Miss Lloyd?' David repeated, gazing round as if expecting to see someone else.

'Ann,' Ricco supplied, looking amused.

Susan's face was scarlet, and she was trying desperately to convey a message to David with her eyes, rolling them towards Vicky in a manner that merely baffled David even further.

Vicky decided it was time she intervened. 'Me, you idiot,' she said, managing quite a convincing laugh. 'I know it's two years since we last met, David, but surely you haven't forgotten me altogether?'

He caught on at last. 'Oh. Oh yes, silly of me—I had something else on my mind, sorry, V . . . er . . . Ann.'

'That's okay, I know how absentminded you are,' she said, wishing Ricco Salvatore wasn't listening with such keen attention. She had a feeling he hadn't missed David's second slip, and was no doubt wondering what David had been about to call her before he corrected the name. 'Do sit down, David,' she added to distract Ricco. 'You make me feel nervous, standing there like that!'

David sat down next to his wife and Ricco

clicked finger and thumb, softly summoning the wine waiter.

'Signor Salvatore?' the man enquired, bending towards him with a smile.

'What will you have to drink, David?'

'A Cinzano rosso, thanks.' When the waiter had moved away David said stiffly, 'Kind of you to suggest that we should be your guests, Ricco, but I insist that you must be ours. You're very welcome to join us, but . . .'

'I tell you what, David, this time you're my guests, and next time you and Susan can ask me to dinner, then honour will be satisfied.' Smiling coolly as though that settled the matter, Ricco looked around. 'Now, where are those menus? I don't know about you, but I'm starving. I've had a difficult day—Bianca is a wonderful creature, but she can be very exhausting.'

Vicky's brows rose. She could believe that. Ricco caught her eye, and a wicked comprehension flashed across his lean, tanned face.

'Naughty, Miss Lloyd . . .' he murmured. 'I can't go on calling you that when you're my guest—may I call you Ann?' His gaze wandered over her in her vivid yellow dress, lingering on the low scooped neckline with an appreciation which brought a faint wash of pink back into her face. The man had a sensuality which needed no words; Vicky felt his blue eyes as tangibly as caressing fingers, and stiffened.

David said irritably, 'We don't call her Ann, we call her Vicky.'

There was a silence during which Vicky and Susan looked at each other across the table and

Ricco glanced from one to the other of them with sharp interest.

'Really? Why?'

David floundered, and Vicky came to his rescue. 'It's my second name, and I prefer it.' The truth was the opposite; Ann was her second name, which was why she had invented her alias that morning when Ricco asked Susan what her name was.

Ricco considered her, head to one side. 'Vicky ... Ann ... mmm ... yes, I think you're right— Ann is a little too simple for you.'

'I don't look simple?'

His smile was derisive. 'Oh, I don't think so.'

The head waiter arrived with the menu a second later, and for quite a while they were all preoccupied with choosing their meal. When the question of food had been settled Ricco and David began to discuss the wine list with the serious faces of men for whom wine is one of the more important elements of life.

Vicky kicked Susan under the table and when her cousin looked at her made an eloquently relieved face. Susan grinned. So far any real problem had been averted.

'I think Vicky should taste the best local wine,' Ricco was saying. 'They have some superb Chianti *riserva* in the cellar.'

While they waited for their first course to be served they talked lightly, largely discussing what Vicky should see while she was in Florence. Several times new arrivals walking past their table halted to greet Ricco. Each time the women in the party kissed him, each time he kissed the lady's hand. Vicky watched, her mouth wry. He had charm; no doubt about that. Well, Miller had been strong on charm too, but he had been as weak as water in most other ways. From now on charm was going to be right at the bottom of her list of desirable qualities in a man. Looks weren't important, either. She had learnt that character was the only thing that mattered. It would be a long time before she looked twice at any man, but when she did she knew what she would be looking for—and it wouldn't be either charm or good looks.

Over their *antipasto* Ricco asked Vicky how long she planned to stay.

'Until Susan and David throw me out,' she said, laughing. 'Well, for a couple of weeks, probably.'

'For as long as you like!' Susan insisted. 'Mustn't she, David? After all, she's practically my sister . . .' Her voice trailed off as Ricco's head lifted, and he stared at her.

'Your sister? I thought you said she was an old school friend?'

Poor Susan was scarlet again. She was not a good liar; lies embarrassed her, she forgot what she was supposed to have said, and sooner or later her tongue tripped her up.

'We were very close,' Vicky said. 'Best friends, just like sisters.' She wasn't going to let Ricco cross-examine Susan.

'How touching,' Ricco responded drily, and she felt like throwing something at him.

'This wine is delicious,' she said instead, changing the subject.

'You haven't got a sister, have you, Susan?' he asked, though, undistracted.

'No, I was an only child,' said Susan, happy in the

security of the absolute truth.

Vicky fished a morsel of something soft and white out of her *antipasto* and waved it at him on a fork. 'What's this?'

'Squid,' he said, and she dropped it.

'Squid? You mean, those things with all the tentacles?' Her face wrinkled in disgust, and Ricco laughed.

'Try it, you'll like it.'

'I don't think I'll bother, thanks.'

He leaned over, picked up the piece of squid with his fork and offered it to her. 'Try it.'

Vicky reluctantly parted her lips and he pushed the food into her mouth. She chewed while he watched her, then mimed surprised pleasure. 'It isn't bad either—you're right.'

The shrewd blue eyes held a spark of sarcasm or derision. 'I'm so glad you agree,' he drawled, as if he knew perfectly well that she had made all that fuss solely to get his mind off Susan's little slip.

The meal was eaten in a leisurely atmosphere in the elegant restaurant. It was obvious that they were expected to take their time and enjoy the extraordinarily good food and wine. Everyone else was doing the same; laughing and talking between courses, sipping wine, looking around, exchanging small talk with neighbours at another table. Vicky hadn't known a great deal about Italian cuisine before she came here; the only food she associated with Italy was pasta in rich sauces. Tonight she was eating a subtle meal, beautifully cooked and varied, more international than she had expected. To her amazement it was well past eleven before they had finished and were drinking their coffee, and she noticed David secretly looking at his watch. Susan noticed, too.

'We ought to be going soon, David has to be at work by eight. People over here don't have the same working hours that we have at home, Vicky. They take about three hours off in the middle of the day, for lunch and a siesta, then go back to work around three-thirty or four. In the summer it's far too hot to work between twelve and four. It can be a hundred in the shade here.'

'That must limit your leisure time,' said Vicky, doing her best to drink her very hot coffee but only getting her tongue burnt.

'I'm sorry to rush off like this, Vicky,' David said, smiling wearily. 'I can hardly keep my eyes open after ten o'clock these days.'

'Look, why don't you two go on and let me bring Vicky home later?' suggested Ricco. 'Give her a key, then you can go up to bed without waiting for her.'

Vicky had an immediate jab of alarm. 'Oh, that's okay, I'm ready to go now, this coffee's too hot to drink.' She began to get up, but Ricco caught her wrist.

'Nonsense! You don't want to leave so early.'

David was on his feet, his face visibly relieved. 'If you're sure you don't mind, Ricco? I don't want to spoil Vicky's first night in Florence, but I need a good night's sleep.'

'I'm delighted,' Ricco assured him. 'I won't keep her out too late.'

Susan handed Vicky a key and reluctantly she took it, realising that it was pointless to argue since both her cousin and David looked so pleased that the problem had been amicably settled. They had felt guilty about breaking up the evening so early.

'Have fun,' they said, hurrying away, waving, and Vicky sank back into her seat, feeling trapped.

Ricco eyed her with amusement, reading that expression. 'I don't bite,' he promised.

'I wish I could be sure of that.' Her voice was cynical and his brows rose.

'Don't you trust me?' He looked round, summoning the waiter. 'A brandy for me.' He glanced at Vicky. 'Will you have a liqueur with your coffee?'

'No, thank you.'

The waiter moved off and Ricco gave her a dry smile. 'Want to keep all your wits about you, do you?'

'Am I going to need to?'

'Not on my account,' he said smoothly, but she wasn't very reassured.

'Florence is a beautiful city, isn't it?' she said politely. After all, it was his city, he was probably very proud of it.

'You haven't seen her at her best. By the time we walk back to my car the moon will be up; it's full tonight, and the city looks lovelier by moonlight than it ever does by day. You won't get a chance to see the streets so empty at any other time—too many tourists, too much traffic. I'm glad I don't live in the city itself, I think I'd have a problem with invasion of my space.'

She stared blankly. 'Parking space, you mean?'

He laughed. 'Personal space.' He moved his hand lazily, describing a circle around himself. 'Don't you know that we all feel we have a force-field around us, keeping other people at a distance, giving us a tiny strip of private territory to walk about in?'

'That's an interesting theory. Is it yours or did you borrow it?'

'I didn't invent it, no. I think it's generally accepted.' He leaned over and ran a hand down her bare arm. She stiffened, the tiny hairs on her pale skin bristling at the contact.

He smiled mockingly at the affronted stare she gave him. 'You didn't like that? I was invading your territory and you objected, you see.'

'My objections had nothing to do with territory, private or otherwise,' she said through her teeth. 'I'm like the fruit on the barrows in the street out there—you can look, but don't touch.'

His eyes wandered calmly. 'Oh, I've been looking,' he said. 'And I like what I see.' His eyes smiled, an invitation in them which she didn't need to know Italian to understand. 'You have skin like a peach; the English often do, it must be all that rain.'

'That's a myth; it doesn't rain every day in England. It's just that we have very changeable weather; we can have four seasons in one day.'

'Englishwomen seem to share the same tendency,' he drawled.

Vicky gave him a cool smile. 'If you're talking about me, I assure you you're wrong. I shan't change my opinion of you, so don't waste any time expecting that I will.'

'I hesitate to ask what your opinion is,' he said wryly, and she offered him another of her cool smiles.

'I shouldn't.'

There was a disturbance around the entrance,

someone had just arrived and was causing a sensation. People were craning their necks and buzzing like a hive full of bees. Vicky curiously looked that way, her mouth tightening as she saw who had walked into the restaurant.

'Well, this is lucky—Bianca's here, I'm sure you'll find her much more appreciative than I am. You can show her Florence by moonlight—she'll love it. I suppose I can get a taxi home if I ask the manager to find me one? I wouldn't want to drag you away just as Bianca arrives.' She stood up, smiling politely. 'Thanks for the gorgeous meal.'

'I promised Susan that I'd see you home safely,' he protested, getting up too.

Bianca was shedding a fur wrap and giving vent to the now familiar stream of excited complaint. Tonight she was in what she no doubt described as a simple little black evening dress. Satin and apparently cut to use the minimum of material, it left nothing of Bianca's luscious curves to the imagination. The bodice plunged at the front almost to her midriff, a modicum of decency preserved by the delicate fan of black lace stretched from one side to the other. Her full, smooth white breasts strained at the lace as she swept down on them, apparently not even seeing Vicky, but gesticulating excitedly as she kissed Ricco.

'*Caro, come stai? Vorrei un bicchiere di vino.*' She settled herself at the table with a rustle of skirts. A bemused waiter appeared with a glass, another bottle of wine, a menu card.

'Sit, sit, sit,' ordered Bianca, tugging at Ricco's arm.

He said something in Italian, gesturing to Vicky,

who was wondering whether to walk away or make some polite pretence of greeting the other woman. As Bianca had ignored her she felt like doing the same, but Ricco was obviously talking about her, so she stayed.

Bianca glanced at her, raised incredulous eyebrows, ran her gaze over Vicky, pouted those full red lips and shrugged. It was a brilliant performance. Vicky was inspected and dismissed with that final amused shrug. It was clear that Vicky was unimportant. She could find her own way home. Bianca brushed her off and sipped some of her wine, smiling at the waiter.

'*Bene.*'

He bowed reverentially, and melted away. Bianca put out a commanding hand to Ricco, giving him an imperious frown. 'Ricco, *caro*!' She patted the seat next to her, but he didn't obey.

Vicky decided she had had enough of the charade. She walked away, leaving them together. She hadn't particularly cared whether Bianca said hallo to her or not, but it had made her hackles rise to be inspected insolently, then dismissed with a shrug. Bianca might be a famous opera singer, but that didn't give her the right to act as though she owned the world. No doubt she did own Ricco, as much, that was, as any woman would ever do. He didn't look the faithful type—he reminded Vicky of Miller far too much. Men could be divided into types; Miller and Ricco had a great deal in common, not least their looks and their sublime self-confidence. Not to mention the way women fell for them like ninepins.

She saw the man she supposed to be the head

waiter, and tried to catch his eye to ask him to get her a taxi, but as he moved towards her Ricco's hand gripped her arm and she turned round, startled.

'I told you, I'm driving you home,' he said, looking impatient.

'I don't want to take you away from Bianca.'

'A very feline remark.' His mouth twisted mockingly.

'Was it? Sorry. I'll get a taxi, there's no problem.' She was irritated to be told that she sounded catty. Why should she care if he stayed here with Bianca? If he spent the whole night with her? She couldn't care less, and if he imagined for one second that she was jealous he could think again.

'You will come with me,' he said, sounding very Italian suddenly, and since several waiters were now hovering within hearing distance Vicky had no option but to let him steer her out of the restaurant.

As they walked in search of his car, she tried to correct the impression she appeared to have given him.

'I simply meant that I wouldn't want you to offend Bianca by leaving her alone there. After all, I suppose she was joining you.'

'She is meeting a number of friends, they will be arriving any minute,' he said coolly.

'I suppose you can always go back there when you've dropped me,' said Vicky, hurrying.

'Where's the fire?' Ricco asked drily, his long legs keeping pace without difficulty. 'You aren't even looking at the moon.'

She threw a glance upwards; the moon was certainly spectacular, and as they emerged on the

Lungarno she saw the silvery flakes of light rippling on the quiet surface of the river, turning the ancient buildings and bridges into a magic city floating like a dream under the moonlit sky.

She was so absorbed that she nearly fell over Ricco when he stopped to unlock his Lamborghini. He turned and steadied her, an arm going round her. Vicky stiffened and backed, and got a dry, ironic stare.

'Talking about myths——' he drawled.

'Were we?'

'Earlier, remember, you said that it was a myth that it always rained in England? Well, it's also a myth that Italian men make passes at every woman they meet.' He held the door of the car open and, flushing, she slid into the passenger seat. Ricco walked round to get behind the wheel.

'They only make passes at the ones they fancy,' he added as he started the engine.

Vicky laughed and he gave her a teasing smile. 'I'll remember that,' she said.

He switched on the tape player fitted into his elaborate Star Wars dashboard, and a voice floated out. Vicky was impressed by it, although she wasn't a great Verdi fan. She guessed who it was, of course, before Ricco said softly, 'Now you know why Florence adores Bianca. She has a voice that can steal the soul out of your body.'

Vicky watched his profile from behind the cover of lowered lashes as they drove away with a purr of enormous power. Had Bianca stolen his soul? Or just his heart?

# CHAPTER THREE

OVER the next few days Vicky and Susan did a great deal of sightseeing, but as the weekend approached Vicky insisted that if she didn't have a day off from tramping around Florence she would scream, so they spent the Friday morning sunbathing, ate a picnic lunch al fresco on the lawn behind the villa, and relaxed.

At three o'clock Susan gave a sigh and looked at her watch. 'I ought to do some shopping, but you needn't come. Stay here and enjoy the sun while you can. The weather may change any minute—it's still only April.'

Vicky lifted her head sleepily. 'Are you sure?' Her ankles still ached from all the walking on Florence's narrow, hard pavements. She would much rather stay here idly, but Susan was her hostess, and she felt obliged to offer to go shopping with her.

'Certain.' Susan got up, smiling cheerfully. 'It will be much quicker and easier if I do the shopping on my own, and I expect you could do with some time to yourself. I won't be long, Vicky. Help yourself to a drink if you want one while I'm gone. Anything I can get you in town?'

Vicky shook her head, smiling back. 'I've got all I need, thanks.'

When Susan had gone Vicky drifted into sleep. The sun poured down, not hot enough to be uncomfortable, yet warm enough for her to have put on one of her bikinis. The cypress hedge round Susan's pocket-handkerchief garden stirred gently, whispering, in a faint breeze; birds sang and bees hummed somewhere among the shrubs and rose trees.

A soft clinking sound woke her, and she languidly opened her eyes to find Ricco Salvatore kneeling beside her, so close that for a second they were staring inches apart. Vicky got the distinct impression that he had been about to kiss her, and jerked upright, twisting her body out of reach.

'If you've come to see Susan, she's out.' Did he often drop over during the afternoon, when Susan was alone and David was at work? That would certainly explain Susan's uneasiness about him and the scowl that appeared on David's face every time he saw Ricco.

'I didn't come to see Susan. I came to see you.' He leaned over to pick up something which turned out to be an elegant glass pitcher of orange juice. Vicky realised that the ice in the pitcher had made the clinking noise which woke her.

'Where did that come from?' she asked, puzzled. Was Susan back? Or had Ricco gone into the villa and helped himself to the drink? Admittedly he was the landlord, but it seemed a little high-handed.

'I brought it with me.' He was pouring her a glass of juice; small squares of ice slid from the pitcher with a chink. 'I saw you out here from my house and thought you looked hot.'

'How thoughtful!'

Her dry tone made his mouth twist and the blue eyes gleam with impatience, but he handed her the glass without retorting.

She sipped, her brows lifting as she felt the tingle of champagne on her tongue. 'It's a Buck's Fizz!'

'Don't you like champagne?'

'Love it. I'm just not in the habit of drinking it in the middle of the afternoon.'

'Try living dangerously.' His eyes roamed and she stiffened on the red and white striped lounger, feeling that exploration as if caressing fingers were sliding over her bikini-clad body.

'I've tried it,' she said tersely, swivelling to take down a gauzy beach jacket from the back of the lounger. She had designed the material herself; a creamy background on which were splashed vivid summer flowers, scarlet poppies, purple anemones, dark blue irises. She slid into it while Ricco watched. It was too transparent to make much difference; he could still see the pale curve of her body through the fine material, but it was a gesture which made it clear that she did not like the way he was staring at her, and it made her feel slightly less exposed.

'I'm intrigued,' drawled Ricco, pouring himself a glass of Buck's Fizz and stretching out on the grass beside her as if he intended to stay for hours. 'Tell me more.'

She sat up, her knees drawn upwards and her chin resting on them, the glass in her hand. 'About what?'

'This dangerous living of yours—what went wrong?'

'I didn't say anything had gone wrong.'

'You didn't have to. I can read between the lines.'

'I'm afraid you're reading things that aren't there.'

He lazily shook his head. 'Oh no, you're on the defensive . . .'

'I am not!' She had flushed angrily at that, and his smile mocked her.

'Oh, you mask it as attack, but only because you believe that attack is the best form of self-defence!'

'You're too clever for me,' Vicky said bitingly, and drank some more to give herself time to think. He was shrewder than Miller had been, but he still reminded her of Miller; less good-looking and with a stronger bone structure, perhaps, but the two men had one quality in common, and they both had it in abundance—charm, a lighthearted, casual panache with which they faced life, certain it would give them whatever they wanted because it always had. Miller had been a star right from the first picture he had made in his early twenties. Ten years of stardom and everything that went with it—money, power, women—had spoilt him. He might have been a more admirable man if he hadn't had all the pleasures of life handed to him on a plate.

'I gather Susan's been showing you around Florence all week,' Ricco said, watching her frowning face intently. 'I came over several times, but you were both out.'

She looked at him, eyes narrowed. 'It must be nice being rich enough not to have to work.'

No wonder David resented and disliked him! While David was working long, hard hours in his office every day, Ricco had all the time in the world at his disposal to come over here with pitchers of Buck's Fizz, flirting with Susan and making the most of his opportunity, as her landlord, to take advantage of her isolation in a foreign city. Susan's only friends were the wives of men who worked with David, and the one thing the women had in common was their men. Vicky had already realised that Susan was lonely. Had Ricco discovered that months ago? Susan loved her husband, but she saw too little of him during the week. David didn't get home until late in the evening most weekdays. Susan was human and Ricco was a very attractive man; his attentions must be flattering. She might feel guilty, but even her guilt was revealing—she wouldn't feel it if she wasn't secretly attracted to Ricco.

'What makes you think I don't work?' His blue eyes were hard with anger, she suddenly realised; they watched her with hostility.

'Do you?' What did he do, then? Was he a director of some company, a sinecure job that took up little of his time?

'I couldn't afford not to!'

She glanced around her, smiling scornfully. 'You have plenty of land here and an enormous house, I assumed you had a private income to go with it.'

'I inherited the estate. I could sell it and raise a considerable sum, but it's been in my family for hundreds of years. I don't feel I have the right to let it go to strangers. That's why I built two villas in the gardens—the rent from them helps to pay for the upkeep of the rest. The house was in a terrible condition when I inherited. It needs a total modernisation—new roof, replastering, up-to-date plumbing—it will take years to get it all done, and it will eat up most of my income.'

'So what is your job?' She drained her Buck's Fizz and leaned down to place the glass on the tray he

had brought over with the pitcher and glasses on it.
Ricco's eyes watched the movement and she
straightened hurriedly, realising that he had been
staring.

'I run a recording company.'

Her eyes widened. 'Really? What's it called?'

'Musica Dolce.'

'Sweet music?' She had been picking up the odd
Italian phrase during the week from Susan. 'That
must be an interesting job—did you start the
company or . . .?'

'I founded it, yes.' He stood up with the tray in his
hand. 'Would you like to see my house? Come and
look over it.'

'Now?' She looked down at herself, face wry.
'Like this?'

'Why not?' he teased, smiling.

'I'd rather change first.' She slid off the lounger,
the gauzy robe flying open, and Ricco brushed a
hand across her midriff, making her jump.

'You've caught the sun there—you had better put
some lotion on it before you dress, or it will be very
uncomfortable later. It isn't wise to underestimate
the sun here—it may only be spring, but you can still
get sunburn if you stay out in it too long.'

She turned away without answering and went
into the empty villa, her skin tingling where Ricco's
fingers had touched it. The little gesture had
reminded her of something she would rather
forget—the night when it had first dawned on her
that Sunny fancied her and was going to make an
embarrassing nuisance of himself unless she did
something about it quickly.

Running upstairs, she tried to forget all about

that, but as she stripped off and put on a white vest top and a pair of pale blue cotton pants her mind was busy with unhappy memories.

She had been alone in the hotel suite in Paris where Miller was staying. Sunny had whisked her over for the weekend, but she had refused to stay in the suite he and Miller were sharing. She had insisted on a room of her own. Miller had been sweet-tempered about it at first, but Sunny had, as usual, been sneeringly sarcastic.

The following morning she had gone along to the suite to have breakfast with Miller, an arrangement they had made the previous night. She had found Sunny alone. He had told her that Miller was taking a shower and would be out in a minute, but Miller hadn't put in an appearance, and eventually Sunny had told her with one of his malicious smiles that Miller had left in the middle of the night to visit an old flame who was also in Paris.

Vicky had turned red and then white. 'I don't believe you! Miller wouldn't . . .'

Sunny had laughed and sat down next to her on the red plush couch on which she was uneasily perching. 'Grow up, sweetheart. Last night you said no to him. Miller doesn't like that, he isn't used to his ladies saying no.' He had been far too close and to her shock she felt his hand close over her leg, pushing aside her skirt, his moist fingers sliding upward and inward along her thigh. 'You aren't a virgin, are you, sweetheart? A lovely girl like you can't have got to twenty-three without going to bed with anyone.'

She had thrust his hand away and tried to get up, very flushed and upset. Sunny wouldn't let her go, he held her down by the shoulders, his body leaning over her, his mouth trying to close over her lips while she turned her head away, feeling literally sick. Sunny was not an attractive man; short and a little plump he was at least forty and going slightly bald. Vicky hated his liquid black eyes and sallow skin, the fleshy nose and even more fleshy lips. At that moment he was loathsome to her, and she gasped the truth out.

'I feel sick—let go, let go of me!'

Sunny had been surprised enough to release her, and she had fled. She had made it back to her own room, where she almost threw up before packing her case and going down to reception to check out and book a flight back to London. All the way to Charles de Gaulle airport she had shuddered, and the taxi driver had watched her in the mirror, obviously afraid she was going to be taken ill in his cab.

Miller had caught up with her at the terminal before she boarded the London plane. His concerned, alarmed face had made her burst into tears. Aware of being recognised, of the curious, fascinated stares of other passengers, Miller had put an arm round her and steered her out of the airport, and she had been in such a state that she had forgotten all about her luggage, already bumping along the conveyor belts towards the waiting plane. A limousine was waiting. Miller put her into it and they drove back to Paris.

'Darling, Sunny didn't mean to scare the life out of you—he was only playing around, he didn't mean what you thought he meant. Sunny's got a crazy sense of humour, and he isn't used to girls like you.

The sort of girls Sunny knows will go to bed with anyone at the drop of a hat, he isn't on your wavelength.' Miller had stroked her hair and kissed her wet face. 'He'll apologise on his knees for upsetting you, I promise you. He can't get used to the idea that I'm going to marry you, Vicky. Up until now we've always . . .' He broke off, giving her a quick glance. 'Well, things are different and Sunny will get the picture now.,

'He . . . he said you were with an old flame last night,' she had half said, half accused, watching him, while she pretended to be drying her eyes with his handkherchief.

Miller looked blank. 'He was just kidding. I was asleep in bed. He woke me up after you ran out of the suite and told me the two of you had had a row.'

'A row?' she had erupted. 'Is that what he called it? He had his hands all over me, he tried to . . .'

'I know, I know, he was out of order, but that's Sunny.' He sounded as if he might at any moment start to tell her that the whole episode had just been a joke and where was her sense of humour?

She hadn't been watching where they were going, and when the limousine stopped and she saw that they were back at the hotel she had turned pale again. 'I don't want to see him—take me back to the airport, Miller!'

He was already getting out of the car. He turned and pulled her out, too, protesting. Vicky hung back, shaking her head, her hair ruffled, her face smudged with tears. That was when the flashbulbs exploded, that was when the camera men and reporters dashed towards them. Miller had been all smiles; Vicky had been dazed.

'No, our engagement isn't off. No, there's no other woman, Vicky's the only girl for me. Okay, we had a little spat and she was on her way back to London, but we've made it up and everything's fine again now, isn't it, darling?'

In the background Sunny had lurked, watching, his cynical face and knowing eyes sending an icy tremor down her spine. Had his pass at her all been part of some publicity ploy? Had he wanted to stampede her into running so that he could blow it up into a major story? Or had he merely been an opportunist, in several ways, taking the opportunity of being alone with her in the suite, and when she turned him down making the most of that, too, by calling Miller and then the press?

Whichever was the true explanation, Vicky had never felt the same about Miller from that day, and she had hated Sunny. He had been perfectly aware of the fact, but that hadn't deterred him from making oblique advances to her later. She almost felt that it amused him to ask her to dance in public, knowing it would be hard for her to refuse every time, and realising just how much she hated to be in his arms, his hands touching her, his face deliberately pressed against her own. He took every chance he could, putting his arm around her as they walked into a restaurant, patting her behind in a pretence of humour, kissing her when they met—Sunny always took care never to go too far, yet he chose his moments shrewdly, and Vicky felt helpless about the way he manipulated Miller and herself. While she was working she could take refuge in her job, get away from Miller's travelling circus, but Sunny made sure he stopped that bolthole, and once she had no job Miller tried to persuade her to travel with him all the time. She knew what that meant, what it would mean. She would be with Sunny most of the day while Miller worked, and Sunny wouldn't leave her alone. She felt like a fly caught in a spider's web of treachery and intrigue, and the worst part of it was that some of her feeling for Miller still lingered. Away from Sunny he was a wonderful man. Sunny was a corrosive influence on him, she decided, but gradually she realised that she would never win against Sunny. He had been with Miller for too long, and Miller was blind to his real nature.

So she had taken the decision to go for good, and this time she had been secretive about it. Nothing would ever change her mind, but she hadn't wanted to face Miller and tell him so, because he would have called in Sunny, and Sunny would have told the press.

From the moment she met Miller, Sunny had made their love a public affair, although for a long time that hadn't dawned on her because she wasn't aware of all the publicity. She didn't read all the newspapers and magazines, didn't see the pictures of herself and Miller at nightclubs, dancing, kissing, jogging in the park, eating hot dogs in New York, swimming in Miami. When she did see the occasional photograph and story she thought it surprising that people should be interested, but she didn't guess how interested they were until she realised that little snippets of inside information about them both appeared regularly because that was Sunny's job, to make sure that Miller's face and name turned up as often as possible in the media.

Sunny had made that crystal clear to her,

eventually. The more intimate the gossip, the better—if she and Miller had a quarrel over another woman, terrific. If she broke their engagement, then was talked into putting on her ring again, wonderful. If she looked jealous when Miller danced with another girl, Sunny had the story in a gossip column the next morning.

It was distasteful, and Vicky couldn't take any more of it. One of the last straws was when she realised just how many women there had been in Miller's life before they met, and, even worse, that when Miller was tired of them Sunny was always waiting around to take up where he left off. That, at least, was what Sunny implied. She didn't know how much truth there was in it, but now and then Miller let fall unguarded remarks that made her believe Sunny's story.

Since she arrived in Florence she hadn't seen any English or American papers, and she couldn't read Italian ones, so she had no idea whether Sunny had told the press about her disappearance, but she imagined that if he had the story would have died by now. Miller had probably got a new girl-friend in tow; maybe the next one would be tougher and more able to cope with all the pressures of that life style—not to mention the problem of Sunny.

She ran a brush over her hair, staring at her reflection. Ricco was right, she had taken the sun, her nose was slightly pink and her throat was flushed. She hadn't thought that the spring sunshine would have much effect; she must treat it with more respect in future. Like love, it could be deceptive and dangerous.

She went downstairs and found Ricco stretched

out on the lounger, his long, slim body totally
relaxed. He had his eyes shut as she walked up to
him, but although she moved softly he opened his
eyes and smiled up at her.

'You certainly took your time! I began to think
you'd changed your mind and forgotten to tell me.'

'I'm sorry.' Vicky knew she sounded stiff.

He swung to his feet, smiling. 'You look very cool
in that. Blue is your colour.'

'Thank you.' She couldn't hide the frostiness of
her response; she didn't want him to flirt with her or
use that charm he had on tap. She had had enough
of men for the moment; she wanted a little peace
and quiet, a space in which to be herself,
unhampered by other people's demands or expecta-
tions. Her love affair with Miller had been too fast
and furious, and it had gone wrong too badly. Her
skin was tender to the touch, her nerves frayed.

She walked across the garden towards the little
gate which she knew led into Ricco's villa gardens
and he followed, carrying his tray like a well-trained
butler, balanced on one hand. His shadow moved
on the sunny grass and she watched it, her eyes cast
downwards. He moved gracefully, she had to admit,
teeth clenched. He had long, smooth hips, an
athlete's body—muscled shoulders, deep chest, long
legs and an easy, loping stride.

If she had met him a year ago she might have
fallen for him hook, line and sinker, but she was a
burnt child and she feared the fire.

'Does Bianca Fancelli record for your company?'
she asked as they walked through the gate.

'Yes, she's one of our biggest stars.'

Vicky paused, delighted with what she saw in the

courtyard of his villa—rows of enormous terracotta pots containing orange trees, the burnt orange of the clay pots glowing in the sunlight, tapering dark cypresses, cherry trees in blossom and some very old statuettes placed here and there among the trees and shrubs; nude and pale nymphs with cupped hands pouring water into a deep basin in which they stood, Roman matrons in draped tunics, a leering satyr which reminded her at once of Sunny. The sun was lower in the sky now; it made soft dark pools of shadow on the grass and flowers and along the walls of the villa.

'Why do you grow your orange trees in pots?'

'Because we sometimes have severe winters, and the terracotta protects them from the worst frosts. Last year we got bushels of oranges from these, but it all depends on the weather, some years we hardly get any.'

They walked through the main door and Vicky's breath caught in disbelief at the long gallery stretching away in front of them. The walls were plastered, and hand-painted with country scenes and paintings of fruit; they must be very old, for their colours had faded into soft washes, but you could still see very clearly what the artist had intended—luscious cherries, red and ripe, round glowing peaches and green apples, and in the landscapes the familiar cypress and olive trees, the groves and vines of Italy, while cascades of delicately painted flowers hung from the high, arched ceiling some thirty feet above them. Vicky hadn't expected to see such a high ceiling; the gallery must be as high as the roof, she realised, and this must be one of the oldest parts of the house.

Ricco watched her entranced expression, smiling. 'In the Middle Ages, of course, this would have been a whitewashed refectory for the monks. The wall paintings were done during the seventeenth century, during the Arcadian period of Italian art.'

'It's wonderful, incredible—I've never seen anything like it!'

Chandeliers hung at each end of the gallery, the largest Vicky had ever seen, dripping with hundreds of glass pendants arranged in layers like the frills on a circular skirt, with separate swags of crystal at intervals around the globe and one long trail of them falling down below the main chandelier. The blaze of light they gave off when Ricco turned them on almost dazzled. In that radiance she picked out the sheen of gilt on antique brass-handled furniture, the colours of the paintings, the deep polish on the red-tiled floor. There were plants in pots everywhere; bushy fern, wide-leaved rubber plants, flowering African violet.

The whole effect was of a shabby beauty; this was a real home, not a museum—she saw books in piles on cupboards, little curios behind glass doors of cabinets, an umbrella left on a chair, a dog's lead hanging on a hook. The plaster was flaking, the gilt scratched, the furniture a little rickety, but someone had polished that floor until it shone like glass, someone had looked after those plants and cleaned the chandeliers.

'When I was small I used to ride my tricycle up and down here,' said Ricco, smiling nostalgically. 'When it rained, that is—otherwise my mother made me go out into the garden, but I loved it to rain so that I could play in the long gallery. It was much shabbier then; we didn't have much money, and the restoration of a place like this costs a fortune—especially the ceiling and walls. I had them cleaned and touched up a year ago. I won't tell you how much that cost.'

'You must have lots of help to keep the house in this condition.'

He smiled. 'Thank God, yes. I couldn't manage, otherwise.'

'Susan said something about a plan to turn the villa into a hotel?'

'I've played with the idea from time to time, but too much needs to be done to it first. A hotel needs bathrooms and modern public rooms—a bar, a dining-room. At the moment, I only use a fraction of the house. I live in three rooms, that's all I need. I'm having the rest of the place redecorated and modernised bit by bit.' He walked on along the gallery and she followed, skidding on the polished floor. Ricco turned and caught her with one arm, then put the tray down and took her by the hand.

'You'd better watch your step—Giulia believes in polishing until you can see your face, and I can't persuade her it's dangerous.'

Hand in hand they walked carefully until they came to a low arch in the wall through which Ricco led her into a square room furnished as a study, with a desk and bookcases and filing cabinets around the walls.

'I work here when I'm not at my office. I come here to get away from the telephone—my home number is private, and that helps to keep the calls to the minimum.'

He opened a door on the far side of the room and

she followed him into a spacious, open sitting-room
with high, wide windows along the wall opposite. It
was furnished with grey and red striped brocade-
covered chairs and a matching sofa, something in
the style of English Regency furniture, with highly
polished acanthus-leaf decorations on the bow legs
of the chairs. The walls were painted in the same
fashion as the walls in the long gallery, landscapes
in gentle greens and blues, giving her a strange
feeling of not being in a room but in a grove. The
sunlight through the windows moved across the
painted trees and she almost felt them stir, smelt the
flowers painted among the painted grass.

'It's so peaceful,' she murmured, looking around
her. 'If I were you, I'd hate to turn it into a hotel,
hordes of strangers trooping through these beautiful
rooms—could you bear it?'

'I may have to, eventually. The upkeep is too
much for my income. It's either turn it into a hotel
or let it slowly disintegrate. You need a lot of money
for a house like this.'

She walked over to look more closely at the
brocade on the chairs, running an appreciative
hand over them. 'Very classy material; this is
original, isn't it?'

'Nineteenth-century,' he agreed. 'It was màde for
this room, for one of my ancestors, by one of the
best Florentine workshops of the time. A year after
it was installed here your Lord Nelson arrived in
Italy, and there's a rumour that he visited my
family, but there isn't a word of truth in it, we just
tell the story to English tourists to amuse them.'

She laughed, catching the wicked gleam in his
eyes. 'Don't you want to amuse me?'

'I'll think of something,' he promised, and she regretted her impulse to flirt with him and turned cool again, looking down at the chair.

'I've seen material like this in the V. & A. I spent a lot of time there, studying old material, when I was at college.'

'You were trained as a designer?'

'I did three years before I joined the firm.' A sigh escaped before she could stop it, and he picked up on that, of course.

'What made you leave them?'

Sunny, she thought, but aloud she said, 'We had a disagreement.'

'And you have no plans yet for another job?'

'When I've finished my holiday I'll start looking for one.'

'Will it be easy to find one? Are there plenty of jobs for designers of textiles?'

Her mouth wry, she shrugged. 'I might be lucky.'

He pushed his hands into his pockets and lounged there, watching her thoughtfully. The sunlight glinted on his dark hair and showed her the golden tan on his throat, that warm deep colour which seemed imprinted in his skin.

'Ever thought of designing record sleeves?'

Vicky stared at him, startled. 'No,' she said frankly, laughing. 'That's a very different branch of design; I'm into textiles, and . . .'

'Don't you ever take risks, impulse decisions?' Ricco asked with a sardonic little smile. 'I think you might come up with some interesting sleeves. While you're in Florence anyway, why not come along to my offices and see the sort of designs we use, get the idea of how we decide what image we want to get over? I know you've been doing something rather different, but that doesn't mean you can't try something new. I've a feeling you might bring a new approach to it, add a new dimension—if I'm ready to risk it, why shouldn't you?'

# CHAPTER FOUR

'Do you think he was serious?' asked Susan eagerly later that evening.

'Well, he suggested I should visit his office and see the sort of work I'd be doing, so I suppose he must have been.' Vicky was dubious, though. She wasn't sure she trusted Ricco Salvatore, he might have an ulterior motive for offering her a job. It might be interesting to get involved in the music business, though. She was very tempted to accept the offer, so next morning Susan drove her into Florence to keep the appointment Ricco had made with her.

His offices were in a narrow street off the Via Tornabuoni, the most prestigious shopping street in Florence, Susan told her. You could buy beautiful clothes, shoes, or some of the jewellery for which Florence was famous, and the area was crowded with people that Saturday morning. Vicky had never seen such traffic in such narrow streets. Internal combustion was murdering Florence. The weather had changed, as Susan had predicted; a cloudy sky sat right on top of the flat roofs and the air hardly moved; sultry and humid, it clung around the houses, loaded with the smell of petrol fumes.

'I'll have to let you off here because of the one-way system,' Susan said apologetically. 'Take a left turn, then a right.' She looked at Vicky uncertainly. 'Do you think you can find it? There's a brass plate on the door. Musica Dolce, can you remember that? The offices are halfway down on the left-hand side. Oh, maybe I should find somewhere to park and walk back to show you the way.'

They were causing a blockage, and the car behind them began to hoot loudly. Susan threw a look backwards, blushing. 'Oh, dear!'

'Don't worry, I'll find it,' said Vicky, getting out of the car. 'I can see what this traffic is like, I'm not helpless, and Ricco said he would drive me back, so I'll see you later.'

She turned to give a grin and a cheerful wave at the young man in the Lancia behind them who was ferociously hooting his outrage that Susan should be holding him up. He stood up in his open-top sports car and called to her in dulcet-tones, his gesture beckoning, but she laughed, shook her head and walked away.

'*Signorina, signorina, per favore!*' he called after her, suggesting a drive or something rather more intimate in his warm Italian voice, but Vicky kept on walking round the next corner and out of sight and his life.

She found Ricco's offices easily and pushed the door open. She could hear a typewriter somewhere, and followed the sound along a passage. The building was ancient, judging by the crumbling plaster, but when she tapped on a door at the end of the corridor and went into the room she found herself in a modern office, high-ceilinged, with windows along the facing wall, steel filing cabinets and a girl sitting at a desk typing.

When Vicky came into the room she lifted her hands from the keys and smiled, beginning to say something in Italian, too fast for Vicky's shaky grasp of a few phrases.

'*Mi dispiace, non parlo italiano*,' Vicky interrupted, smiling apologetically.

The girl's face cleared. 'You are Miss Lloyd, yes? Please to go upstairs, Signor Salvatore is in the main office. I will tell him you are coming.' She picked up a phone and Vicky turned away. On her way out she heard the girl talking in her own language and laughing at whatever the person on the other end of the line was saying.

Vicky sighed. It was shameful, the way everyone here seemed to speak such good English when she barely knew half a dozen words of Italian. The staircase was narrow and not too well lit, but as she reached the top of it Vicky saw Ricco coming towards her from an open door.

He was wearing a cream linen tailored suit, the shirt he wore with it made of a lustrous apricot silk. His tie was very plain, a dark brown silk, unpatterned. Vicky admired the panache which could carry off the combination; she distrusted the crooked little smile he also wore.

'You're very punctual. I was afraid you might have trouble finding us.'

'Susan gave me very precise instructions,' she answered politely, although she felt the odd little prickle on the back of her neck she always got whenever she saw him.

He ushered her through a door into a high-ceilinged, spacious room which was completely empty of people.

'Oh, nobody else here? Don't you work on

Saturdays?' she asked, looking around her with curiosity.

'Only when I have something important to deal with,' he said drily.

'Am I something important? How flattering.'

His eyes mocked her. 'What do you think of our main office?'

'Very impressive.' She glanced around again, admiring the impression of airy brightness the room gave, even on a day as misty as this; it was a working environment which she could imagine finding very pleasant. Air-conditioning made the long room cool; plants everywhere made it feel like a garden.

There were enormous windows at each end, stretching almost from ceiling to floor. Pale blue venetian blinds covered them, no doubt to shield the workers from the worst heat of the day in summer. It had been designed on the same open plan as Susan's house, divided by low shelving topped with troughs of plants into separate areas, some containing desks and filing cabinets, others with racks of records and stereo equipment with headphones so that one could listen without annoying everyone else.

'I designed it myself.'

'I thought you might have done,' she said drily, and got a wry smile.

'Would you like some coffee? I have some already made,' He walked over to a broad shelf on which stood coffee-making equipment, lifted the pot and poured two cups. 'Milk? Sugar?'

'No, thank you, I like mine black.'

He brought the cups over to a wide, round table in

one of the alcoves and gestured for her to sit down. On the table lay a large portfolio. Ricco handed her a cup of coffee and then flipped open the portfolio.

'Take a look through here, before we talk.'

Vicky pulled the portfolio closer and began to glance through it at the paintings it held, each of them framed in a square of white paper. They differed widely: landscapes, faces, city streets, abstracts. The lettering on them differed just as much; small or enormous, splashed diagonally or written from top to bottom—the artists had gone to great trouble to ring the changes. The concept was, of course, similar to magazine drawing or any other form of commercial art—each drawing tried to illustrate the theme of the record and at the same time catch the eye, surprise, intrigue.

'Fascinating,' she commented when she had turned the last page. 'The technique is simple enough, nothing new to me, but I'm not that sort of designer, Signor Salvatore . . .'

'Ricco,' he interrupted, and she shrugged.

'Ricco, I can see that you have some brilliant artists working for you already, far better than I could ever hope to be. Some of those illustrations are inspired.'

He nodded, pulling the portfolio towards him and opening it again. 'Agreed. This guy, for instance . . .' He showed her one of the best in the collection. 'He's brilliant, yes, but that means he's very much in demand and costs the earth. We can't afford him unless the record is a sure-fire bestseller.,

Vicky gave him a cool stare. 'And you think I'd come cheaper?'

His mouth curled up. 'You're very direct. Yes, I

suppose that's partly it—but it's more than that. It occurred to me that it might be interesting to have sleeves illustrating the typical fashions of the period for a new series of chamber music we're producing—Renaissance music, for instance; you'd have an enormous choice of styles and materials to use there. The series covers five centuries of Italian music. We plan to issue several discs for each century, so we'd probably be talking about ten or a dozen covers in total. As you see, the actual illustration would be drawn much larger, since we need to see the details very clearly and it will be reduced in production.'

She was interested, in spite of her reluctance to have anything to do with him and his scheme. 'It would involve a lot of research in costume museums and libraries, picture galleries, of course . . . and I'm no expert on Italian costume. I might know where to start in England—I studied costume at college, naturally, that was part of my course.'

'I thought it probably had been,' he said smoothly.

She laughed, her mouth tightening with irritated amusement. 'Clever of you. You had it all worked out, just like that, in a flash?'

'That's why I said it was a hunch. I had already had the idea of using costumes of the period for the series, but I'd meant to use famous paintings, not get a modern artist to reproduce the clothes people wore. When I heard that you designed textiles it seemed like an omen. There you were, and there was my project; you clicked together magically.' His blue eyes held a wicked sensuality; he picked up her hand before she knew what he was going to do and entwined their fingers firmly. 'Like that,' he added softly.

Vicky pulled her hand free, her face cold. 'Ah, which brings me to the real reason why I came this morning,' she said, sitting up straight on the other side of the table. 'Susan.'

Ricco looked blank. 'Susan?'

'Have you any idea what sort of trouble you've been making for her?'

'I have? What do you mean? Susan's in trouble?' His tanned face wasn't smiling now, his eyes were fixed on her, frowning.

'You've been flirting with her ...'

'What?' he interrupted, brows a black, angry line above eyes like blue ice. 'I've never ...'

'Kissed her hand? Gazed into her eyes and told her how lovely she looked? Smiled at her across rooms, taken her flowers, called on her in the afternoons while David was at work?'

She had to admit he did the stupefied innocence well. His lean cheeks had taken on an angry wash of red and his mouth was a straight, tense line.

'I'm not in the habit of making passes at young married women,' he said brusquely, barely parting his teeth to let the words out. 'Did she tell you that I'd made advances to her?'

'No, Susan said you couldn't help it, you flirted instinctively with every woman you met.'

For a moment he just sat there, breathing heavily while he eyed her with what appeared to be homicidal intentions, then he gave a snarling sound and said, 'You believe in coming to the point, don't you? *Va bene*. Okay, let's be frank. If Susan got the idea that I've been flirting with her and meant anything by it, please assure her that my intentions towards her were . . .'

'Oh, please!' Vicky couldn't help the laughter which broke out of her. 'Not honourable, surely? And your English is usually so good.'

'My English is perfect,' he said through his teeth. 'I spent three years in your country, after leaving Milan University—a year at Cambridge and then two years working in London with record companies. So don't patronise me, Miss Lloyd.'

She looked down demurely. 'Sorry. But anyway, it isn't Susan who has the wrong impression—it's David, and their marriage is under quite a strain because of you. Susan doesn't have the right sort of temperament to handle a situation like this—David is ten years older than her, and she's a nervous girl at the best of times. She hasn't a clue how to make David realise that he has no cause to be jealous of you.'

Ricco got up and walked away, prowling restlessly, his hands in the pockets of his cream pants. She heard him muttering to himself in Italian; the words sounded fiery, and she was glad she didn't know what they meant.

He stood at one of the wide plate-glass windows staring out, his black head haloed with morning light. 'This is absurd,' he said in English. 'I'd no idea. Oh, I knew David wasn't very friendly to me, but it didn't dawn on me that he was actually jealous, or that there was anything behind Susan's shyness whenever I saw her. Of course, she always blushes and stammers, but I thought that that was her character, that she was simply a very sensitive girl.'

'She is—and with good reason.' Vicky began to tell him about Uncle George's icy sarcasm and the way he flayed Susan with his comments on her looks, behaviour, intelligence. 'So you see, when David flies into a jealous rage she simply dissolves into tears or runs away—she can't face him or discuss it as any sensible woman would. They don't talk to each other like two adults. David makes all the decisions, he's very much master of that house. Susan can't cope with his jealousy of you, she can't convince him she doesn't secretly fancy you because the very subject makes her fly into one of her tizzies.'

He swivelled and leaned against the window-frame, staring at her down the long room, his lean body poised and dangerous, vibrating with anger.

'So you decided to interfere?'

Vicky lifted her chin defiantly. 'I decided to make you see the sort of problem you had caused. Maybe you didn't mean it, maybe you can't help flirting . . .'

'Maybe I ought to throw you out of here before I lose my temper!'

She got up. 'Okay, I'm going, I've said what I came to say.'

He crossed the room in long-limbed strides and caught her before she got to the door, his hands descending on her shoulders and whirling her round to face him.

'Not so fast! I've got a few things to say to *you* now. I'm none too pleased to hear that you and Susan have been talking about me behind my back and deciding that I'm just a shallow flirt who can't keep his eyes off any woman he meets.'

'I didn't put it like that!' His fingers were biting into her flesh, but she didn't dare to struggle; it might inflame his temper further.

'That was what you meant! You made me sound like a conceited fool.'

Their eyes met and his face tightened into rigid, hostile lines. 'That *is* what you think of me, isn't it?' he demanded, shaking her.

'My opinion of you isn't important. It's David and Susan I'm concerned about. I'm very fond of Susan, I want her to be happy, and at the moment she isn't, although she should be. Just stop flirting with her and David will get over this.' She tried to break out of his grip, but it tightened on her.

'I haven't been flirting with her! When I see her I'm polite and friendly, she's pretty and charming and I wanted to make her feel at home here.' He paused, seeing the glint of derision in Vicky's eyes. 'Damn you! Don't you know the difference between a natural courtesy to a woman and making a pass at her?' His blue eyes were glacial, but she could see hot red glints in them and his voice had a metallic ring to it. 'There's more to communication than language. Let's try another way of making the point.'

His head swooped before she could back or turn her face away. His mouth hurt as it took her lips by force; the insistent pressure bruised and burnt, and while she was struggling to escape Ricco's arms encircled her and held her so tightly that she could hardly breathe, let alone break free. She backed a step, but that was no help; she found herself against the end of one of the partitions, and Ricco's body crushed her backwards until she was trapped between him and the solid wood. His muscled thighs leaned on her, holding her immobile, and one hand slid up her back and moved over her short blonde hair, tangling with it until his fingers suddenly closed over her nape, massaging it softly, his other hand caressing her spine, curving her body inwards towards him.

Vicky had kept her eyes angrily open; she had no intention of letting him get to her. What did he think he was doing? The kiss was too painful to be enjoyable, even for him—what did he get out of inflicting it on her other than some balm for his bruised ego?

The movements of his hands gradually undermined her, though. Their warm, firm caress was hypnotic, she found herself growing heavy-eyed, almost drowsy. The power of his mouth softened, he kissed her more as if he wanted to, as if it gave him pleasure, and her lids finally closed as her body arched obediently, her hands closing over his shoulders and clinging there. The sunlight bathed them warmly, the silent room enclosed them, all she could hear was the beating of her heart and his, all she could see was the golden glow beneath her lids.

Ricco reluctantly released her lips and lifted his head. She opened her eyes and looked dazedly at him.

'*That* was a pass,' he said huskily, and she thought she saw mockery in his blue eyes.

That acted like a douche of cold water. She finally managed to break away, twisting her body and moving several feet off, breathing far too fast, her face much too flushed.

She was angry with him—but far angrier with

herself for letting down her defences. What had happened to her determination never to let him get any closer? Hadn't she learnt her lesson over Miller? Ricco was charming and attractive and sexually exciting—which made him all the more forbidden to her. Next time she let herself care about a man he was going to be a very different type, quiet, stable, reliable. Ricco Salvatore didn't fit the bill.

Moving to the door, she flung over her shoulder, 'Don't ever try that again or you'll be sorry!'

She heard his laughter with fury. How dared he laugh at her? She meant it, every word, and she wished she could think of some way of wiping the amusement out of his face, but short of actual violence there was little she could do about Ricco at the moment.

'You enjoyed it as much as I did,' he drawled.

'Like hell!' She turned at the door to glare at him. He was sitting on the edge of a desk, watching her with wicked eyes.

He made a horrified face. 'What shocking language! An innocent young girl like you!'

She fumed helplessly under his mocking gaze. 'I don't think you're funny! Keep your hands to yourself in future, that's all!' She swung round to march out, and he called her back.

'Haven't you forgotten something?'

'What?' she asked shortly, halting in spite of a feeling that she ought to go now while they were a room apart. Those long legs of his could cover far too much ground far too fast.

'When will you start?'

'What?'

'The job—when does your holiday end? How soon can you start work here?'

'You have to be kidding!' Vicky spat out furiously. 'You don't think I'm going to take a job with you when . . .'

'If you want David to believe I'm not interested in his wife, what better way of convincing him than by making him think I'm interested in you?' Ricco asked calmly.

She stared at him, dumbfounded.

'Take a few days to think it over, anyway,' he drawled. 'You can let me know on Monday. If you aren't taking the job I'll have to think of an alternative, so don't take too long.'

Vicky began to walk towards the door, nodding. 'Very well, I'll let you know.' She wanted to get away from him fast.

He followed her. 'I'm giving you a lift back, remember?'

She had forgotten completely, and he saw it in her face and laughed. Vicky set her teeth. She wasn't going to be able to get away from him just yet. She hoped she had done the right thing in tackling him about Susan. Sometimes interference could do more harm than good. When she had gone back to London, Susan would still be here. She hoped she hadn't put any ideas into Ricco's head that hadn't been there before. Even worse, she hoped she hadn't made him hostile to Susan and David. He was their landlord, after all. They enjoyed living in that little villa.

As they drove out of Florence the mist lifted and the sun shone through the clouds. Ricco glanced up at the sky. 'It looks as if it` going to be a fine weekend, after all. What are you planning to do? More sightseeing?'

'David said something about seeing the Tuscan hills.'

'You'll enjoy that. Get him to take you to Fiesole, one of my favourite places.'

'Etruscan, wasn't it?'

'Oh, Tuscany is saturated with the past—but even if you aren't interested in history, Fiesole is delightful. The views are quite incredible,' He glanced at her sideways and she took a deep breath.

'Keep your eyes on the road!'

The Lamborghini flashed along like a rocket now that they were out of the thick chains of Florence traffic, and it made Vicky nervous to have him looking at her instead of at the road.

'Don't be nervous,' he said, smiling, and patted her knee.

She brushed his hand off angrily. 'Will you stop touching me! Wasn't it you who told me that it was a myth that Italian men made passes at every woman they meet?'

His eyes slanted, dark and provocative. 'I said they only made passes at women they fancied, and that's true.' His hand was back on her knee, but he had removed it before she could hit him again, and he was laughing. 'Have you got a hang-up about men? You're very aggressive.'

'Not normally,' she retorted through her teeth. 'Only when I meet a man who makes me lose my temper.'

'Or a man who finds you attractive?' he queried, lifting his brows, and she was furious to feel herself flushing. He watched her, his eyes mocking. 'Now I wonder why you should find that so annoying?' he asked.

'I might be more flattered if I didn't suspect that you find a lot of women attractive,' she snapped. 'There's no particular thrill in being one of a crowd.'

'What makes you think you are?'

She laughed shortly. 'Oh, come on! Every time I see you, the evidence is pretty conclusive. I didn't need Susan to tell me you're a flirt, and I doubt if Bianca is the only other woman in your life.'

'Are you jealous of Bianca?' he asked, sounding amused, and her colour turned scarlet.

'No, I am not! I don't care who you go around with—I'm just telling you why I don't take you seriously.'

'Yet,' he said softly, his mouth curling in a complacent smile.

She turned icy. 'Ever,' she promised.

They were turning in at the gates of the villa now. Ricco slowed the purring monster and smoothly turned towards the front door of the little villa. He braked and switched off the engine and turned to survey her speculatively.

'It's dangerous to issue challenges of that sort,' he pointed out. 'No man likes to back off from a dare.'

'It wasn't a dare. It was a statement of fact.' She opened the car door and got out, and Ricco watched her with narrowed eyes. 'Thank you for the lift back here. I'll let you know about the job on Monday,' she said remotely.

That afternoon David and Susan took her on a drive around the countryside surrounding Florence, passing through Pistoia and into the tiny, remote villages in the hills. Spring covered everything with a vivid green glaze, the sun was warm and the hills beautiful. It was a lovely drive, and Vicky began to get some idea of the landscape surrounding her. They drove back through Lucca to get on to the autostrada, and were back at the villa in time to have dinner at home.

On the Sunday they all slept late, but after they had had a light breakfast of rolls and coffee David drove Vicky into Florence to visit the Uffizi, which was open until one o'clock. Susan preferred to stay at home to prepare lunch. One picture which Vicky found really striking was an Uccello, a Renaissance battle scene crowded with life and incident. It wasn't the people that made her eyes open; it was the fact that one of the horses was blue, strangely prefiguring modern painting. She had seen reproductions of most of the famous paintings in the Uffizi, but this was new to her, and she stood in front of it for a long time.

'What do you like so much about it?' David asked, studying it.

'It surprises me.'

'Is that good?'

'Art should always surprise. Most of us tend to go around with our eyes shut, metaphorically. We don't see what's right under our noses. The job of the artist is to shake us into looking, perhaps for the first time, at the familiar things we pass every day.'

'Like blue horses?' a voice drawled behind them, and she turned with an impatient expression to face Ricco Salvatore.

'What are you doing here?'

'Being shaken by the sight of a blue horse!'

David seemed amused. 'What do you think of the

painting, Ricco?'

'Ask me what I think of Vicky and I'll be more eloquent,' Ricco said, letting his eyes wander over her with cool sexual interest.

'Do you often spend your Sunday mornings in art galleries?' Vicky enquired with scepticism.

'No, I called at the villa and Susan told me you were here,' he admitted shamelessly.

David laughed. Vicky had never seen him look so friendly towards Ricco. Obviously he was far from displeased to see his landlord pursuing Vicky, and Ricco's eyes mockingly underlined the fact as he glanced from David's smiling face to Vicky's hostile one.

'Have you seen the Boboli Gardens yet?' he asked her.

Before she could answer, David said, 'I was just going to take her there—why don't you do the honours? You know them better than I do. Vicky couldn't have a better guide.'

'You're a very good guide,' Vicky said hastily, but Ricco talked over her.

'I'd be happy to. Come along, Vicky. The Gardens are a very popular place to walk on fine Sundays, but people usually crowd in there after lunch.'

'Are you coming, David?' asked Vicky, finding herself being towed away by Ricco's commanding grip.

'I'll catch up with you later,' he said, wandering away to admire some more pictures.

'Enjoyed your morning?' Ricco asked as they went down the wide stone staircase.

'Very much,' she said shortly. He made her feel

hunted. Why had he followed them here?

'Why did you go in for textile design instead of painting?'

She laughed angrily. 'What a question! Because that's what excites me, I suppose—texture, shape, colour. When I see someone wearing a dress made with material I've designed it gives me a kick. It's only when the material is worn that it really exists, flowing with the body moving under it. Then it's a living creation instead of just a design on paper.'

He listened with real interest, watching her excited face. They crossed the Ponte Vecchio and turned in through the gates behind the Pitti Palace, and Vicky looked up with some apprehension at the steepest public park she had ever seen.

'Who had the brilliant notion of making a park on the side of a cliff?'

'You have to be fit to stroll along these paths,' Ricco admitted drily. He led her through the green groves, past statues hidden in niches, the rain having made faint green tearstains down their marble faces; then turned upwards at an incline that took all their energy and left them none for conversation, along a beautiful cypress alley lined with sculptures from many different periods.

At the Neptune fountain he watched with amusement as she caught a few glittering drops of spray in her hand. 'Don't drink it,' he warned, and she gave him a dry look.

'I wasn't intending to. Can we sit down? My muscles are protesting like crazy. If I don't sit down soon my legs may go on strike!'

They found a green bench behind a low box hedge and sat down. Vicky stared at the tender blue sky; below it the flat roofs of Florence massed, and from up here you could see across the city to where the dark blue hills rose like the backcloth of some Renaissance play.

'I wonder where David's got to,' she mused, wishing Ricco wouldn't watch her, he made her self-conscious. She wondered what went on inside his head—why did she have the distinct impression he was plotting something? Or was she being cynical? If she had never met Miller, she wouldn't have been so suspicious of every man she met. She would probably have been a pushover for Ricco Salvatore. She couldn't deny he was sexy. Apart from Miller, he was probably the best-looking man she had ever met, and a year ago she might have given him a firm green light if he made a pass at her instead of angrily brushing him off every time he appeared.

'I expect he'll wait for us at the gate. You could hunt for someone for hours in the Gardens, there are so many different paths up to the top.'

She looked ruefully upwards. 'I hope you don't expect me to walk all that way!'

He grinned. 'No, we'll walk down again when you've got your breath.' He crossed one long leg over the other, turning towards her, his arm going along the bench. 'Thought hard about the job? Made up your mind?'

She shifted slightly so that his hand no longer lay against her nape, and felt his quizzical smile although she wasn't looking at him. 'I'm tempted,' she began, then stopped, making the mistake of glancing uneasily at him.

'Good,' he answered silkily, well aware of what

had just crossed her mind.

'That wasn't an intentional double meaning!' she snapped.

'Don't they call it a Freudian slip?' he enquired.

Her flushed face tightened. 'Look, can we get one thing straight? I'm not interested in you, Mr Salvatore. I might be interested in a job with your firm, but only on my own merits. I don't want you to make one for me with the idea that I might be available for more private duties outside working hours.'

'I could lose my temper with you any minute, Miss Lloyd,' he snapped, suddenly grim-faced. 'Do you really think I need to go to such lengths to get a woman? Or do you merely think that you're so ultra-desirable that every man you meet is going to crumble to his knees at the first sight of you?'

She got up and began marching back downhill to the park gates. Ricco caught up with her at the next bend, but he seemed to have nothing more to say. A few moments later they saw David waiting at the park gates.

'Did you have a good time?' he asked Vicky, then did a double take at the look she gave him. David threw Ricco a bewildered look, and found his profile just as rigid.

'*Ciao*,' he said, bestowing the word between both of them in icy indifference, and walked away. David stared after him.

'Did something happen?' he asked Vicky uneasily.

'Every time I meet that man something happens,' she snapped, and it was only later as they drove back to the villa and Susan that it occurred to her that those words, too, had a double meaning. Her clashes with Ricco were fuelled by more than mere irritation over his disturbing manner. Each time she saw him she reluctantly felt the lure of his attraction. You couldn't disguise that immediate chemical reaction, even from yourself. It was meaningless, of course. She didn't know him well enough for her awareness of him to be more than instinctive and physical. All the same, every time they met something certainly happened, both between them and inside herself. That was what annoyed her so much.

# CHAPTER FIVE

VICKY was awake until very late on the Sunday night, making lists of pros and cons, but she still hadn't decided about Ricco's offer of a job when she came down to breakfast on the Monday morning. She kept veering between a strong desire to accept the challenge of an entirely new sort of artwork— and an equally strong uneasiness about the sexual challenge Ricco presented.

David had left for work before she got up, but she found Susan in the kitchen drinking some fresh coffee and reading the latest issues of the English newspaper which Susan's mother sent out in a bundle once a week to keep her daughter up to date with home news.

'Anything interesting happening back home?' Vicky asked, sitting down and pouring herself a cup of coffee. There was a wicker basket of rolls on the table; she took one and spread it with cherry jam. It was home-made local produce, thick and rich with dark fruit, very sweet.

'Strikes, murders and a train crash—oh, and a picture of the Princess of Wales in her latest hat,' said Susan, offering her the newspaper. 'Don't worry, there's nothing in it about you, I looked.'

Vicky didn't want to read the paper. She pushed it away, grimacing. 'I can't believe that I once used to read gossip columns myself, enjoying all those fascinating titbits about jet set life. It always seemed like real life soap opera. I don't think I actually believed any of the gossip, but I had no compunction about reading it.'

'Well, famous film stars don't seem to have real emotions, do they?' Susan said. 'Some of them get married four or five times. No wonder people stop believing they can get hurt like anybody else!'

'Those like Miller can't,' Vicky said tersely. 'Their lives aren't normal. All the money in the world can't make up for turning into a bit of flotsam floating on top of very murky waters.'

Susan looked horrified. 'Oh, poor Miller! You're very hard on him.'

'Don't be so soft-hearted. He's chronically incapable of being faithful to one woman, and he's as weak as water.' Vicky got up impatiently. 'Didn't we decide to go to Fiesole today?'

'Yes, of course. I'll be ready in two minutes,' Susan agreed, clearing the table. Vicky helped to load the dish-washer, admiring the compact way in which the kitchen had been designed. Ricco was really very clever. He must have a very clear, tidy mind. She found that slightly worrying, somehow.

Fiesole lay on the crest of a conical hill, looking down towards Florence and the river valley. Driving up towards it Vicky got a glimpse of some of the beautiful landscape she had been gazing towards from Susan's garden, those misty backdrops so like the distant perspectives of a Renaissance painting, green and grey, with cypress trees making dark exclamation points against a blue sky.

'It's a very old city,' Susan told her in between taking the curling bends in the steep road. 'Etruscan—much older than Florence. They had a

war, actually, in the Middle Ages some time—
twelfth century, I think. Florence won and sacked
Fiesole, and after that it was Florence which
dominated Tuscany, but I love Fiesole because it's
small and gives a feeling of being open and
spacious, because it's on a hill, I suppose. You get
the feeling you're up in the sky.'

'*I* get the feeling we're going too fast!' said Vicky,
clutching the door as Susan swerved round another
bend.

'Sorry,' said Susan, slowing.

Vicky stared out of the window at the villas one
could see on each side of the road, appearing and
vanishing behind trees just breaking into blossom.
They seemed to be built of the same stone as the
houses in Florence, and were often the same colour,
their paintwork faded by the hot Italian sun, their
roofs the typical orange-red.

'What a super place to live! The views must be
terrific.'

'They are. Lots of famous people have lived up
here, it's a favourite place for the rich and powerful
to settle down. Even the Medicis had a villa, just
outside Fiesole. It isn't open to the public, it's
privately owned, but it's gorgeous, so I'm told.'

They parked quite close to the small town centre
and walked around the main square, the Piazza
Mino da Fiesole, which they found from their
guidebook had been the site of a Roman forum. It
was lined with trees, the pavements crowded with
street cafés and tourists like themselves. Vicky
bought a few Etruscan reproductions, a small
bronze owl and a tiny greeny-blue horse. She let
Susan talk her into visiting the Roman theatre and

walking up the steep hill to see the Duomo, a thirteenth-century church. When they walked down again Susan wanted to shop around for a set of fruit dishes, modern versions of a Roman model. The shops seemed to vary in price and it paid to check on them, but Vicky's feet were aching again, so she sat down at a café on the very edge of the hillside, looking downwards over the terraces and fields to the Arno valley, while Susan went to do her shopping.

A boy brought her an iced citrus drink, fresh squeezed lemon which was refreshingly tart on the palate. She leaned back in her chair in the sunlight, sipping her drink and watching the crowds, the lovers hand in hand, the pink cherry blossom on a nearby tree, a cloud passing over the busy square.

A woman at the next table was reading an English paper. Vicky glanced at the front page idly—and then froze. A picture of Miller covered half the page, and under it ran a black headline followed by a column of print. It was the headline that hit Vicky: MILLER OSBORNE CAR CRASH. She leaned forward to try to read the opening words of the story, but the woman holding the paper shifted, giving her an indignant glare, so that Vicky could no longer see that page.

Tense and disturbed, she took another sip of her lemon drink, looking round to see if she could catch sight of Susan. She wanted to get back to Florence as soon as possible now. She must get hold of a copy of that edition of the paper, and they were unlikely to find one in Fiesole. The kiosks in Florence sold English papers, however. The papers Susan's mother had sent had been days out of date.

'You look very grim on such a lovely day!'

She stiffened at the sound of that increasingly familiar voice, looking up in disbelief. 'Are you following me about?'

He leaned over, his hand on the back of her chair. 'Not this time. It's sheer coincidence.'

'Oh, of course!'

His eyes laughed. 'Fate meant us to meet.'

'Fate can mind its own business!'

He bent closer, and she ducked her head under his arm and out of reach. Ricco shrugged and moved away, dropping into the chair opposite her. She didn't like the calmly patient expression in his face, the look of the fisherman whose fish has ignored the bait, but who is prepared to sit there all day waiting for it to come and be caught.

'I came up here to see one of our studio engineers who was taken ill during the night. It wasn't serious, but he has a weak heart and I was worried when I heard he was ill. He ought to retire, but Giorgio is a stubborn man and doesn't want to give up working.' The cherry tree behind Vicky's chair cast a dancing shadow across his face as he gestured, for once very serious. 'We don't want to lose him, either, but I keep a close eye on him to make sure he doesn't overdo things. If it's his job or his health, his health has to win.'

'Is he better this morning?' she asked sympathetically.

He shrugged. 'If you believe him, yes. His wife looked very tired. I think she has to carry a lot of the worry. Giorgio isn't the worrying type.' He looked at her glass. 'What are you drinking?'

'Iced fresh lemon. It's delicious.'

The waiter had been hovering for a few seconds. Ricco ordered two more of the same and leaned back in his chair, crossing his long legs. The woman at the next table was unashamedly staring at him over the top of her newspaper. Vicky felt like telling her to keep her eyes to herself; it was infuriating the way women stared at him. Men had never watched her the way women seemed to watch Ricco. No wonder he was so conceited and sure of himself! All his adult life women must have been tumbling into his arms at the slightest encouragement.

'Are you up here alone?' Ricco asked

'No, Susan's with me but she went shopping. She should be back any minute.'

'Did you tell her that you'd spoken to me about her?' he asked drily, and she flushed.

'No, it would have sent her into a tizzy.'

'It didn't exactly make my day, either,' he drawled. 'I've thought over what you said, and although I don't accept that you were right . . .'

'I didn't expect you would,' she said bitingly.

'Although I don't accept your version of my behaviour,' he growled through his teeth, frowning, 'I'll make very sure in future not to give her the wrong impression.'

'Thank you,' she said, and looked away, down at the valley, her eyes absently tracing the undulations of the landscape. The colours here were so gentle, and yet so vivid; the leaves had a newly minted clarity against that soft, misty blue sky.

The waiter brought their drinks and Vicky glanced back at Ricco. He was looking around the open-air café thoughtfully. She saw his eyes meet those of the woman at the next table, who immediately smiled at him. Ricco smiled back, a faint, wry little smile. He knew, of course, that the woman had been staring at him for some time. How could he help knowing?

The woman got up and came over to the table. Incredulously, Vicky watched her smiling at Ricco again. 'Would you like to borrow my paper? It's yesterday's, but I heard you speaking English and thought you might like to catch up with the news from home.'

Vicky's heart missed a beat. If Ricco saw that story about Miller, he might put two and two together. She hadn't told him her real surname, but simply reading about a girl called Vicky who had disappeared might make him start to think, and he was clever. She knew he hadn't missed her occasional slip, that he was curious about her and her odd reticence about herself.

'That's very kind of you,' he replied, giving the woman a charming smile and accepting the newspaper. 'My wife and I will enjoy reading it.'

He put the paper on the table and Vicky discreetly pulled it towards her and pretended to glance at it. In fact she was watching Ricco and the other woman, who had begun to back, rather pink, obviously taken aback by Ricco's lie about having a wife.

'Well, nice to meet you,' she mumbled, and fled. Vicky's cold gaze followed her. Talk about being obvious! She didn't see herself scraping acquaintance with a good-looking man in that shameless way.

Pushing the newspaper hastily into her shoulder bag, she met Ricco's ironic eyes.

'It must be your fatal charm,' she told him.

'To which you're impervious?'

She smiled sweetly and didn't answer.

'Give it time,' he said coolly, then looked over the table. 'What happened to the newspaper?'

Vicky's eyes shifted away, and at that second she caught sight of Susan on the other side of the road, just going into a shop. Vicky stood up and made a big performance out of waving, but Susan wasn't looking that way.

'That's odd,' muttered Ricco, glancing down around the table. 'What on earth happened to it? Did it blow off the table? I'd swear I put it down right there in the middle.' Obviously he had been too busy watching his departing admirer to notice Vicky concealing the paper in her bag.

Vicky thought desperately of some way of distracting him. 'About that job,' she said and he looked at her attentively.

'You'll take it?'

'I'm not sure—Susan tells me it isn't easy to find a flat here. And then there's the problem of getting a work permit.'

'No problem, I can handle that. As to somewhere to live, I have a suggestion to make.'

Vicky couldn't help the cynical smile. It annoyed him.

'Don't jump to conclusions!'

'I'll try not to.'

'I could easily learn to dislike you,' Ricco said impatiently.

'Start now,' she invited.

His eyes held a flicker of aggressive hostility, but he smiled tightly. 'If you'll let me explain? My house is enormous, as you know, and I only live in part of it. There are many rooms which are empty although they're perfectly habitable. One wing could be used as a separate apartment. The rooms are small. They were the monks' cells originally; they're pretty basic, whitewashed walls, stone floors. At the moment they're empty, there's no furniture in them, but I have plenty of that. The house is crammed with old furniture, so you can take your pick. You'd have your own front door, too. The wing is quite self-contained.'

She stared at him, taken aback. The problem of where she would live if she did take the job had been one of her main reasons for hesitating. She certainly couldn't impose on Susan and David for ever. The house was too small, and they had a right to privacy in their own home.

'You and Susan would be neighbours, you could see her quite often,' Ricco coaxed. 'She seems to be rather lonely here, she'd like to have you living near by.'

'You've thought of everything,' she said drily.

His smile was complacent. 'Have I convinced you that this is an opportunity you shouldn't miss?'

'Whose opportunity, though?' she enquired.

His eyes held intimate mockery, and she felt the back of her neck prickle with sharp awareness of him. He was a man whose sexual impact was immediate and inescapable, even on women who weren't exposed to his deliberate charm. Vicky didn't want to make the mistake of getting involved with him. She had only just escaped a similar trap. Angrily, she wondered why she kept meeting men like Miller and Ricco. She must give off the wrong

vibrations. Did Ricco think he was getting some
sort of signal from her, and was that why he kept
pursuing her? Some women did play a tricky game,
on the surface indifferent while underneath they
were inviting male interest. How was she to
convince Ricco she wasn't one of them, that she
wasn't pretending to run while constantly looking
back to make sure he was following?

'Stay in Florence, Vicky,' he said suddenly, his
eyes holding hers, and she stiffened, her mouth
going dry. He was far too attractive; she ought to
get away while she could.

Susan arrived breathlessly while they were
staring at each other in silence. She fell into a chair,
clutching her parcels.

'Oh, I'm so thirsty!' Only then did she realise
Ricco was sitting opposite her cousin and a flush
invaded her face. 'Oh, Ricco—hallo, I didn't see
you there.'

'Hallo, Susan,' he said politely.

Vicky pulled herself together. 'Did you get what
you were looking for?' she asked her cousin.

Susan nodded and began to talk about the items
she had bought. Ricco called the waiter and ordered
Susan a glass of mineral water.

A few minutes later Vicky looked at her watch.
'Shouldn't we be going, Susan?'

Susan nodded, getting up, and Ricco rose, too.
'Let me know your decision before tonight,' he said,
calling the waiter over to pay the bill.

Vicky nodded. 'See you later, then,' she agreed.
'I'll come over to give you a final decision this
evening.'

As they walked away, Susan asked, 'Is he talking

about the job?'

Vicky nodded, her face wry. 'Yes, and he's offered me a place to live, too. Guess where?'

Susan paused beside her car, looking enquiringly at her.

'In his house!' Vicky said drily.

'No!' Shocked, Susan stood there, the door half open. 'He didn't make a proposition, Vicky? What a nerve! He's only met you a couple of times. I'm surprised you didn't smack his face!'

'He put it very discreetly—said there was an empty wing in his villa I could use, old monks' cells, he said, and I could pick out my own furniture from other rooms. I'd have my own front door and be very private.' Vicky got into the car and laughed angrily. 'He must think I was born yesterday. I'd move into his house one day and he'd move into my bed the next. He can think again!'

Susan slid in beside her. 'There is an empty wing, mind you. The rooms are small, little stone boxes, in fact—he showed it to us once. In winter they're freezing, there's no heating in that part of the house, but in summer they must be beautifully cool—the walls are so thick.'

They drove down to Florence in a stream of other cars. Fiesole was a popular place for visitors and Florentines alike. Susan said that locally people believed it was cooler in Fiesole in summer than it was down in the closely packed, dense streets of the city. On summer days people headed out of Florence up into the cool hills, leaving the sweltering, dusty streets behind them for a few hours.

'Not to mention the traffic,' Vicky said wryly as they came nearer to Florence and the cars became a traffic jam, hooting, bumper to bumper, the air full of petrol fumes.

As soon as she could get away she went to her own room, sat down on the bed and got the crumpled newspaper out of her bag, hurriedly turning the pages until she found Miller's photograph. She read the story anxiously, on edge until she realised with enormous relief that the headline had been misleading. She should have known it would be—popular papers always tried to dramatise the trivial.

Miller had crashed his car while he was driving on a country road late at night. He had been drunk and run off the road into a tree. By some lucky fluke his injuries had been minor, a few cuts and abrasions, a bruised rib and possible concussion. His seat belt had saved him from going through the windscreen.

Sunny had talked to the press, brushing aside the questions about Miller's blood alcohol level. Yes, Miller had been drinking heavily, he had admitted, but only because he was distraught over losing Vicky. They had had a lovers' quarrel, she had walked out and Miller had been out of his mind with grief.

'My God,' Vicky muttered through her teeth, screwing up the paper, 'how can he lie like that?'

She walked angrily to the window and back again, tense as a caged animal. Only when she had begun to calm down did she start to think sensibly. Sunny's press release hadn't simply been aimed at blackening her; he had been getting Miller out of trouble, giving a believable explanation for the drunken driving, which otherwise might have serious consequences. If the police prosecuted,

Miller might be heavily fined—he might even be sent to prison.

Sunny was shrewd and knew how to manipulate the press and public opinion. He was making a fuss over Vicky's disappearance and Miller's alleged heartbreak in order to distract attention from the drunken driving. Of course, the press had leapt at the wider dimension of the story like hungry trout jumping at crumbs. It made a routine drunk driving into a headline story.

Thank God Ricco hadn't seen the paper. She stared through the trees at the roof of his house. The car crash would intensify press interest, keep the story alive. She couldn't go back to London while she ran the risk of being recognised.

She had to take that job. It was her only chance of staying away from England until Miller went back to the States and the story died down.

That evening Susan asked her if she was going over to see Ricco before dinner or afterwards.

David looked up from the newspaper he was reading. 'Are you dating Ricco?' he asked curiously, smiling.

'No, he's offered me a job, and I said I'd give him my answer tonight.'

'I thought you'd turned that down?'

'I'm having second thoughts,' she said evasively.

Susan told her husband about the apartment Ricco had offered Vicky in his villa, and David's eyes widened.

'He obviously fancies you,' he laughed, clearly relieved at the thought that Ricco Salvatore's amorous attention was straying from his wife. 'Well, I'm sure you can handle that,' he added.

'After coping with a Hollywood big shot surely an Italian businessman is no problem?'

'No problem at all,' Vicky agreed, her face rebellious. She wasn't going to admit that she found Ricco Salvatore any sort of threat.

'That wing of his house isn't super comfortable, though,' Susan pointed out. 'It's rather stark and basic.'

'That doesn't bother me,' Vicky protested. 'It sounds quite modern—simple living with a minimum of frills!'

'Then what have you got against the idea?' David asked reasonably, and she couldn't come up with an answer.

That evening, while David and Susan were watching *Dallas* on television—the famous faces talking in fast, hard-to-believe Italian—Vicky went across the garden to call on Ricco to discuss the idea of working with him. She was almost persuaded that it would be a good idea, but first she wanted to see the rooms in which she would be living. She wandered past the orange trees in their enormous terracotta pots and rang the bell on the main door. There was no answer for several minutes, and she was about to turn away when she heard the click of high heels along the red-tiled floor of the long gallery. Through the glass of the door she saw Bianca Fancelli, swaying languidly on her high-heeled white sandals, her lovely figure glittering in a scarlet and gold lamé dress, the impact of which was only heightened by the fact that some of it was missing. Bianca opened the door and regarded Vicky through smouldering eyes.

'*Si?*'

Vicky couldn't help staring at the smooth bare golden midriff, against which dangled swinging, gleaming tassels of gold suspended from Bianca's breasts.

'Er . . . *mi scusi*, Signor Salvatore, *per favore*?' she mumbled, lowering her eyes, but that didn't help much, because now she could see the long slits at the thigh which revealed more of Bianca's beautiful skin.

'*Cosa vuole?*' Bianca demanded, and went on to say a lot more in her furious Italian before Vicky got a chance to say it didn't matter.

'*Non importa, grazie.*'

There was little point in seeing Ricco Salvatore tonight. She couldn't compete with Bianca for his attention, especially not in that dress. Vicky turned away and walked back, telling herself that anyway Bianca had looked like a circus performer with all that glitter and nakedness. She and Ricco Salvatore suited each other!

# CHAPTER SIX

VICKY was drinking a second cup of coffee at the breakfast table next morning when someone rang the door bell. Susan got up and went to answer it. Vicky heard her voice change, heard the deep warm voice which answered, and looked towards the hall with a frown. Ricco walked in and eyed her drily.

'*Buon giorno, come sta?*'

'*Sto bene, grazie,*' she said, tight-lipped, and his brow lifted.

'Did you get out on the wrong side of the bed?'

'Would you like some coffee, Ricco?' Susan intervened quickly.

'I'd love some, thank you,' He sat down at the table, without taking his eyes off Vicky. 'So, what did you want last night? Why did you go away again without seeing me?'

'How do you know I called?'

'I saw you from the loggia—we were drinking coffee up there. By the time I got downstairs you had walked off—Bianca said she'd told you she would fetch me.'

'In Italian, maybe, but I don't speak your language. And anyway, I thought you probably had your hands full.'

Her dry tone didn't go unnoticed. 'Bianca and I were working,' he said impatiently.

Her mouth curled. 'Oh, sure.'

'You have a very suspicious mind!'

'A mathematical one,' she said, drinking some more coffee. 'I put two and two together, that's all.'

'Or, in this case, one and one?' he enquired, his blue eyes very dark.

'Well, I didn't need a computer to work it out,' she agreed. 'I didn't want to interrupt anything, so I left again.'

'You wouldn't have been interrupting anything.' He glanced across at the kitchen area where Susan was making some fresh coffee. Raising his voice a little, he called to her, 'Oh, please, don't bother just for me, Susan!'

'It's no bother, I expect Vicky will want another cup, and the old pot was quite cold.' She came towards them with a clean cup and saucer and put them down on the table. 'It's a lovely morning, isn't it? It won't be long now before summer arrives.'

Through her lashes Vicky watched Ricco's uptilted black head, his skin lit by sunlight, the clear-cut profile striking. He smiled at Susan without any of the teasing he normally showed her, and Susan smiled and walked back into the kitchen.

Looking back at Vicky, he said, 'Last night, Bianca and I were . . .'

She cut in sharply. 'Look, what you do in your own home, in your own time, doesn't interest me! Your private life is entirely your affair.'

'We were working!' he insisted, his voice rising. 'And I didn't like the way you used the word affair.'

Vicky was irritated with herself. She was beginning to sound like a jealous woman, and Ricco wouldn't be slow to decide that that was just what she was. It wasn't true, of course; she wasn't jealous of Bianca. If any other woman had opened that door last night she wouldn't have been so annoyed, but there was something about Bianca Fancelli that infuriated her. The singer was too sure of herself. Too sexy, too beautiful—too everything! Vicky thought venomously. Bianca made her feel insignificant, mousy, dull.

Susan came back, face anxious, to pour his coffee, and Ricco gave her another of his careful smiles. At least he wasn't flirting with Susan any more.

'I'll start tidying the bedrooms, I think,' said Susan. 'Excuse me, Ricco.' She vanished discreetly upstairs. Ricco sipped his coffee, watching Vicky's expressive face.

'If you've stopped quarrelling with me, can we discuss the job?' he asked sarcastically.

'I've decided to accept the offer,' she replied stiffly, and saw his smile with resentment. He needn't look so pleased with himself. She wasn't taking it to be near him.

'Come over to the villa now and I'll show you the apartment,' he suggested.

She called up to Susan, who appeared at the top of the stairs, a duster in her hand.

'I'm going over to Ricco's villa to see the rooms,' Vicky told her and Susan nodded, looking relieved that they were in a more amicable mood. Argument always upset her.

As they walked across the gardens, Ricco asked mockingly, 'Do I get a prize?'

She stiffened. 'For what?'

'Treating Susan like a maiden aunt.'

'Virtue is its own reward.' She turned innocent eyes on him. 'Is Bianca still at your house?'

He opened his front door and stood back for her to enter. 'She and her manager had dinner with me last night, then they went back to their hotel.' He paused, eyes teasing. 'There's no need to be jealous.'

'I wasn't!' she snapped, taking an unwary step. She had forgotten how highly polished the floor was. Her feet slid from under her and she would have crashed to the floor if Ricco hadn't caught her.

She suddenly found herself lying across his arm, splayed like a rag doll. Off balance, she looked up dazedly at him.

'I've got you where I want you now, haven't I?' he murmured wickedly, his mouth curling in a smile of sheer mockery.

Vicky's eyes flickered restlessly and her colour rose, but she wouldn't let him know how disturbed she was by the way he was watching her.

'You won't get me anyhow, anywhere,' she assured him through tight lips. 'Let go of me at once.'

He made as if to do so, and at once her feet slid again and she gave a gasp of alarm, clutching at him.

'I thought you wanted to get away from me?' he said lazily, skimming his gaze over her flushed face until he was staring at her mouth. Stupidly, Vicky felt her heart skip a beat. It was shock; that was all, she told herself.

'Help me to stand up,' she ordered sharply, her hands moving up to his shoulders, while she tried to avoid looking at him.

His hands closed on her waist and lifted her upwards. She was furious with herself as she found she was watching his face in spite of her firm intention not to. His skin was so tanned and clear, a smooth, dark gold. The line of his mouth had a strangely hypnotic fascination. You could read his character in it; a strong will, humour, even, oddly, a certain detachment. He was not a man to treat lightly; he was a lot less obvious than she had thought, and, perhaps, far more likeable—but if he kissed her she would hit him.

He didn't. He dropped his arms and stood back, watching her through his lashes. Vicky was surprised—and it showed. She saw a quiver of amusement run through his face. Furious, she turned and walked off along the gallery. Ricco kept pace with her wary steps, halting at an arched door in the wall. He produced a key and unlocked the door.

'This is the only way through to the empty wing, so this would be your private front door,' he told her with a sideways smile of derision. 'So you could be sure of privacy.'

She made no comment, following him along a narrow whitewashed corridor off which opened a row of doors. Ricco opened them one after the other so that Vicky could see the rooms. They were just as he had described them—square, whitewashed, empty.

The final one was a bathroom, apparently from the Victorian era, with a vast white enamelled bath and a lavatory of the same period enclosed in polished mahogany.

'My grandfather had the bathroom installed,' he told her, turning on the taps in the bath. The water came out reluctantly and was rather rusty, but after it had run for a while it cleared.

'It's a museum piece, but it works,' he added, turning the taps off. 'I'm afraid there's no heating in these rooms, but I can get an electrician in to put some points in strategic places.'

'What about cooking?'

'I could have a simple kitchen installed within a week—an electric stove, a sink, a few cupboards.'

Her forehead creased. 'All this would be very expensive, surely?'

'I've been meaning to have something done with this wing for a long time. When you leave, I could let this place to someone else.'

'You said something about furniture,' she reminded him.

'Come and choose what you like.' He took her round the closed rooms of his villa, opening shutters to let the sunlight into dark, stuffy bedrooms often crammed with furniture from a strange mixture of periods. Vicky knew very little about antiques, but she could see that some of the pieces must be very valuable, whereas others were merely old.

It was rather fun, like shopping with a blank cheque, able to pick whatever you fancied without worrying about the cost. She didn't like to risk choosing anything that she suspected might be worth a lot of money, so she largely concentrated on Victorian and Edwardian pieces—a brass bed and a wardrobe and a tiny kidney-shaped dressing-table of polished oak for her bedroom, a pink-velvet-covered chaise-longue, and two matching chairs for the sitting-room. Ricco persuaded her to add a stained glass Tiffany lamp with a solid brass base, a nest of tables in black oak, a small bookcase and a few other items.

It was obvious that a large part of the villa hadn't been kept dusted and cleaned in the way that the rest of the house had been. Ricco showed her most of the rooms, some of them revealing signs of damp. The upper rooms had crumbling plasterwork, and their ceilings were cracked and dirty. The air in them was musty.

'It seems a shame to let these rooms decay like this,' she said to Ricco, who nodded agreement soberly.

'When I can afford it, I'll have the whole place modernised, but my company profits go back into the business at the moment.'

Some of the older pieces had been homes for mice; she saw stuffing leaking out of chairs, horsehair littered under a sofa. When she ran her hand over a sideboard her finger came away coated with pale dust. Yet she gained an impression of spacious elegance at times, a glimpse of an age long vanished, chandeliers glittering from stuccoed ceilings, deep-piled carpets and brocade and silk. Paintings hung on the walls—she had no idea if they were valuable or not, but some of them were of men and women with Ricco's features: high, arrogant noses, black hair, eyes that stared with his cool assurance, mouths shaped like his and jawlines full of Ricco's determination and insistence.

'My grandfather,' he told her when she stood and stared at one of them, a portrait of a typical Victorian, she decided—upright, dressed in sober dark clothes, a white shirt with a stiff collar rising against his throat. He had all the family characteristics except that his direct eyes were black, not blue, but she felt that his mouth was a little cruel, a thin upper lip and a lower one which combined sensuality with a certain fierceness, and gave his high-boned nose the look of a beak, the beak of a bird of prey.

'He looks rather daunting,' she observed.

'He was an old devil. My father was petrified of him when he was in a temper. He ran his household with a rod of iron, but then in those days I suppose men did.' He gave her a sideways glance, gleaming with mockery. 'The good old days!'

'Which you regret, of course!'

'The days when women knew their place and men ruled the world? Doesn't everyone?' He was laughing, but she frowned.

'I wish I thought it as funny as you do, but I get a little tired of masculine jokes about women's place being in the home and men being superior. In a way, I think I preferred it when it wasn't said as a joke, when men meant it seriously—at least that was honest. Now they make jokes about it to your face and secretly mean it, and that's worse.'

'You prefer honest tyranny to a secret hankering after it?'

'At least you know where you are with it when it's out in the open. You can fight it then.'

'Hasn't anyone told you—the fight was over long ago, the war's ended.'

'Then what was all that stuff about the good old days?'

'You have no sense of humour,' Ricco told her, and Vicky eyed him scornfully.

'I don't like black jokes, I admit, or sick ones. My sense of humour is limited to what's really funny.' She looked back at his grandfather.

'What was your grandmother like?'

'Small, frail, beautiful—even when she was eighty, which is when I remember her best. She was only four foot ten, but she had more spirit than a wild horse. I don't think my grandfather frightened her. In fact, my mother always told me it was the other way round—*he* was scared stiff of her.'

'Good!' Vicky said ferociously, and Ricco took her arm and steered her out of the room on to the wide loggia on the upper storey of the house. She had long ago lost count of the number of rooms there were or the number of staircases she had been up and down. The house was built in the most rambling, ramshackle way imaginable; Ricco said that there had been additions to it from time to time over the centuries. At one period it had been occupied not only by his family but by a dozen servants, with their wives and children. Now Ricco had two people working for him—a woman who did the housework and a man who looked after the gardens.

The loggia was just a wide terrace with a low wall topped with smooth plastered columns facing outwards. On the terracotta tiles stood pots of geraniums in flower, red and pink and white. The sun made patterns on the floor and whitewashed walls. There were half a dozen wicker chairs arranged along the loggia. They were a golden colour in the sunlight, their cushions a pale green weave.

'It's charming,' said Vicky, entranced, and wandered along to the other end, gazing out through the columns at the gardens and the other houses she could see through some clumps of pine trees and oleanders.

'I'll have all your furniture moved in there during this week. I should be able to get the electrician along over the next few days, then the place will be ready for you. When will you start work?'

'I'd like another week's holiday, if that's okay with you?'

'*Va bene,*' he said, joining her, his shoulder touching hers as they both leaned on the parapet of the loggia and stared at the blue spring sky.

'You have no family, Susan tells me.'

She looked round, sharply. 'Did she indeed?'

'You don't like to talk about your family?' Again he sounded faintly Italian.

'I don't like people discussing me behind my back.'

'I asked about your family and Susan told me,' He gave a wry Latin shrug. 'What's wrong with that?'

'When was this?' When had he seen Susan alone since she arrived? Her eyes darkened with suspicion as he watched her, and his mouth compressed impatiently.

'I rang her, early this morning, to find out if you had plans to go out today or whether I would find you in if I came over after breakfast. And you can stop looking at me like that—what am I being accused of now?'

'Oh, nothing,' she said, flushing. 'My parents are dead and I was an only child. Susan is my closest relative, except, of course, her mother—and she isn't a blood relation. My father was Susan's father's brother. They're both dead now. Susan and I practically grew up together, we're more like sisters than cousins.'

Ricco was staring at her oddly. 'I thought you were old school friends, not cousins.'

Vicky stared back at him, dumbstruck. She had completely forgotten lying to him, and now she had been caught out.

'What other lies have you told me?' Ricco asked, and she bit down nervously on her inner lip.

'None,' she managed in a whisper.

'Why lie to me about being Susan's cousin? I don't understand. Why couldn't you tell me the truth in the beginning? What was the point of making up that fairy tale about being at school together?'

She clung to the edge of the parapet, trying to think. What could she say to him? How could she talk her way out of this?

'I . . . I was irritated with you,' she said slowly. 'It was a silly joke, that's all.'

'Oh, that's the sort of humour that really amuses you, is it?' His tone was biting. 'Telling lies for no reason—an odd way to behave, isn't it? Or is this another lie? Is there more to this than I understand yet? Why did you come here? For a holiday or to get away from something? Are you in some sort of trouble? Is that it?'

She swallowed, and he caught hold of her arm and turned her back to face him, his cool fingers digging into her arm. She was wearing a short-sleeved blue tunic top and a pair of pink cotton pants. Suddenly she found herself shivering as though it had turned cold.

'Why did you leave your job in England? Were you dismissed? You might as well tell me—it won't take me long to find out anyway, you know. I can easily check on your last job—perhaps I should, to get a reference,'

At that she turned on him, her head flung back and her eyes angry. 'I'm not desperate for this job, you know. It was your idea, not mine. If you've changed your mind about it—well, that's fine with me.' She pulled free and began to walk away fast.

It was a full minute before he came after her, and by then she was at the foot of the stairs leading down to one end of the long gallery. As she began to walk towards the front door, she heard Ricco running down the stairs. She was afraid to move too quickly in case her feet skidded again on the polished floor, and Ricco rapidly gained on her, his long legs covering the ground at twice the speed of hers.

He caught up at the door. 'Don't turn temperamental on me! I didn't say I'd changed my mind, only that I was curious about your reasons for lying to me. Is that so odd? How would you feel in my place?'

'Maybe it wasn't such a good idea for me to take this job, though,' she evaded. 'I know nothing about this sort of artwork and I . . .'

'You've accepted the job. I'm holding you to that.' His voice was cool and hard; his face matched it. She looked up warily at him. Why was he so determined that she should work for him? And what if he did check up with her previous employer? That would really put the cat among the pigeons. She should have thought of that, but Florence seemed so far from London, this was another world, another life.

'I don't want you getting in touch with my last firm,' she insisted, and saw the tightening of his features, the hardness of his eyes.

'No? Why not?'

'I haven't done anything criminal, I'm not on the run from the police, but I don't want my old boss to know where I am, I don't want him to find me.'

Ricco's eyes narrowed, probing her face. 'I see.'

She looked down, sliding her hands into the pockets in her pants. 'He'd come to find me, and I don't want that. It's all over, but . . .'

'He won't accept that? You had an affair with him?'

Flushed, she shrugged.

'He's married, I suppose? Older than you?' Ricco's voice was icy and contemptuous. 'And you suddenly came to your senses and walked out, but he still wants you?'

She risked a glance at him through her lashes. 'You won't get in touch with him, will you? Please! I couldn't go through that again, you don't know what it was like.' The truth came into her shaky voice at that moment; she was talking about Miller and Sunny, although he didn't know it. 'Please, don't interfere—I don't want this job if it means getting in touch with him again.'

She heard Ricco breathing, a rough, ragged sound, as if he was bitterly angry. She was beginning to guess that he was old-fashioned in some ways—you could say more kindly that he was a traditionalist. He might flirt with a married woman, but he didn't approve of girls who had affairs with married men. Well, neither did Vicky, but she didn't have double standards—one stan-

dard for herself and another for everyone else.
Ricco obviously did, and she despised him for that
and resented the way he was staring at her, the
distasteful twist of his mouth. It had thinned and
tightened; suddenly it looked very much like his
grandfather's—that cold, cruel mouth which had
struck her so forcibly in the portrait upstairs. He
had no right to look at her like that. Even if she had
been telling the truth, she would have resented
having judgement passed on her by a man who was
almost a stranger.

'Do you still love him?' he asked harshly.

Vicky flung back her head and looked him in the
eye. 'No.' She answered honestly. No, she no longer
loved Miller, she knew she never had. There was a
gulf between the sort of crazy, excited feeling she
had had for Miller and real love. That was deeper,
more fundamental, surely? It didn't grow like a
mushroom at first sight and wither almost as fast.

Ricco held her gaze. She found the fixed lance of
his stare slightly unnerving. What was he looking
for in her face to stare like that? Some proof that she
was telling the truth this time? Or was he trying to
work her out? They barely knew each other, after
all. He had acted on impulse, offering her this job
and rooms in his own house. Was he beginning to
regret leaping before he looked?

'But you were in love with him once?' he asked,
his mouth hard.

She looked away. She wished she hadn't lied to
him in the first place; it had been done on crazy
impulse, a desire to hide her real identity. When
they met at the airport, she hadn't known whether
or not Susan had ever mentioned her to Ricco,

talked about her cousin's engagement to Miller Osborne. It would have been quite natural if she had, Miller was famous, it would have been the sort of information one does mention in passing conversation.

'Answer me,' Ricco said tersely, and she reluctantly looked at him again.

'I suppose so, in the beginning.'

His eyes bored into her, making her even more nervous. 'So that explains your prickly mood ever since we met,' he said as if to himself. 'Once bitten, twice shy, is that it?'

She decided it would be wiser not to answer that; he was very close to the truth.

'I'm sorry I lied to you,' she said huskily. She did regret lying, but she knew that if the situation recurred she would have to behave in exactly the same way, because it was a choice of evils. Whatever happened she couldn't bear to have Miller, Sunny and the press on her trail again.

'I wish I understood you, Vicky Lloyd,' he said slowly. 'Is that even your name?' He watched the little start she gave, his mouth compressing. 'I see it isn't.'

'It is Vicky,' she muttered.

'Well, that's something, I suppose. Why can't I know your real name? Are you famous? Would I recognise your real name, is that it?'

She closed her eyes, giving a sigh. 'There's no reason why you should recognise my name,' she evaded. 'I simply didn't want to get involved with anyone in Florence. I was trying to forget.'

'Oh, you made it crystal clear that you didn't want to get involved,' he said through his teeth. 'And now

I understand why. You've just broken off an affair with another man, and don't want to risk any new relationship.'

'Something like that.' She was surprised by the strength of her own regret. Why should she feel so upset because Ricco looked at her with cold contempt and disappointment?

'I presume you really are a trained commercial artist?' Ricco asked drily. 'You can do this work I'm offering you?'

'Oh, I can do it,' she said in a low voice. 'If I can't you can always fire me.'

'I will,' he promised, almost as though he hoped he would get the chance.

# CHAPTER SEVEN

A WEEK later she moved into the apartment, which looked quite different once it held furniture, warmer, smaller, more homey. The spring was in full flood now, and with all the windows open, soft air blew through the rooms and sunlight picked out the gleam of polished wood. Vicky invited Susan and David to Sunday lunch that weekend. She didn't cook, she served salad and cheese and fruit, but it was fun eating the food in those new surroundings.

Susan lay on the pink velvet chaise-longue, sighing. 'I feel like one of those languid Victorian ladies—where are my smelling salts?'

'You ought to have a house-warming party,' David suggested, inspecting the plumbing in the bathroom with incredulity a few minutes later. 'This is the oldest bath I've ever seen outside a museum! I must take some photographs of it, or people will never believe it!'

It was an enjoyable day, and when they had gone back to their villa Vicky sat by the open window looking into Ricco's garden feeling idle and contented. It was the last day of her holiday—next day she started work in Ricco's firm. She hadn't seen much of him over the last few days; he had been in Rome on business, but his housekeeper, Maria, had supervised the builders, and had helped Vicky to move in that weekend. Maria was fifty, plump and cheerful and sang off key as she worked.

She spoke English when she felt like it, which wasn't very often, but her broad smile said more than enough. She and Vicky got on at once. The kitchen wasn't yet completed, which was a snag. 'Lazy swine,' Maria told the men with a friendly smile. They didn't seem to take it amiss, promising fervently that it would be finished by the middle of the next week.

*'Va bene,'* said Vicky, and the men all laughed over their glasses of rough red local wine. They didn't take tea breaks; they took beer breaks or wine breaks, but they got the work done, and the kitchen was beginning to look very good.

Vicky had a strong feeling she was going to be very sorry to move out of this apartment. She could sit here by this window forever, looking into the garden and watching dusk falling over the orange trees and grass, listening to the poignant calls of the birds.

A new sound made her look upwards, startled. Bianca was leaning on the low wall of the loggia, talking over her shoulder in a throaty purr. She was wearing something black and off the shoulder; her bare skin gleamed like gold silk as she beckoned. Vicky eyed her with dissatisfaction; her magnificent body was tawny and dangerous in that dress— why did she always wear such daring clothes if not to show off that incredible figure?

A second later Ricco appeared beside Bianca and Vicky shot back from the window, her heart performing a strange acrobatic leap. She hadn't seen him for a few days, that was all; it was odd that at the sight of him she reeled back as if she'd had an electric shock.

Her nerves jangled violently; she sat down on a

chair, wondering what on earth was wrong with
her. She could still see Ricco through the heavy
cream lace curtains over her windows. His tanned
face was in profile; the combination of gathering
dusk and seeing him through the lace made him
more than ever reminiscent of his Victorian
grandfather, a long, arrogant nose, hard mouth and
insistent jaw. He was wearing a black evening
suit—obviously he and Bianca were going somewhere special.

Vicky felt a sharp little stab of emotion—
annoyance, distaste, she told herself. It couldn't be
jealousy. Why on earth should she be jealous? She
hardly knew the man.

She stayed out of sight; she didn't want Ricco to
think she was spying on his love life, or that she was
interested in what he did. He had denied that there
was anything but business between himself and
Bianca, but Vicky didn't believe him. She knew
what liars men were, and she couldn't believe that
any man could be indifferent to that tigrish figure,
those languorous, provocative eyes. Bianca reeked
of sex; even her voice held the musk of sensuality.

She was murmuring in Italian to Ricco, her body
half-turned his way, swaying invitingly towards
him, her breasts visible above the black satin of her
dress.

Vicky watched Ricco's expression, her mouth
tight, teeth clenched together. So he wasn't Bianca's
lover? Then why was she putting her arms round his
neck? Vicky got up to walk away, she didn't want to
see them kissing. She felt like a voyeur already. She
should have turned her back on the window the
minute she saw Bianca on the loggia.

She went to bed early that night because she had

to get up very early. Ricco had promised to drive her to work, and he would be picking her up at seven-thirty.

Waking in the pale dawn was something of a shock to her after the lazy days in the sun. She felt half asleep even after a cool shower. She dressed carefully in a cool blue linen dress with white shoes. Her mirror showed her the image she was after—a capable professionalism. She didn't want Ricco's staff to get the wrong impression. She wouldn't be surprised if they had jumped to the conclusion that she was Ricco's girl-friend—even Susan and David seemed to believe that his motives were purely personal.

Vicky eyed herself threateningly. If Ricco had given her this job because he hoped to have an affair with her, he could forget it. She had no intention of letting him lay a finger on her.

Do you hear that? she asked her reflection, but her mirrored eyes seemed to hold a knowledge which she found disturbing.

She turned away as she heard Ricco's tap on her outer door. He was precisely on time; it was seven-thirty, she saw when she looked at her watch.

She opened the door, feeling intensely nervous. Ricco's dark blue eyes flicked down over her slender figure and she saw his mouth twist.

'Very cool,' he mocked. 'Settled into your new home? Maria tells me the builders haven't finished the kitchen yet—I apologise, I'll see them about that later today and try to prod them into hurrying themselves.,

'No problem,' she said offhandedly. 'I won't be cooking while the weather is so fine.' She followed him out of the villa. 'How was Rome?'

'Hectic as ever. You need a course of vitamins before you can face the place these days. It gets more crowded every year.'

It was easier to talk to him than she had feared—but then Ricco didn't know she had seen him last night with Bianca, so *he* wasn't selfconscious with *her*.

He opened the door of his car and she slid into it, prickling as he watched her slim legs swing sideways. Sometimes he reminded her so much of Miller, as now, when he gave her that intimate, teasing smile, his eyes gleaming behind their thick black lashes. Why should she feel edgy just because she had seen him with another woman? If he had a dozen women it meant nothing to her.

Perhaps she was jealous because of the humiliation of discovering that Miller was dating other women while he was engaged to her? Her ego had taken quite a beating at Miller's hands. She was scared stiff of a repeat performance.

Ricco's gleaming Lamborghini made short work of the drive into Florence until it met the usual clogged traffic jam inching its way into the city.

Ricco had his window wound right down. He leaned out, his body graceful in a lightweight white suit, gesticulating impatiently, when the car in front hesitated about moving off from some traffic lights.

He sank back in his seat, muttering in fierce Italian, then caught her eye and grimaced. 'Traffic like treacle this morning—I wonder we put up with it. What sort of life is it when we spend so much time sitting in tin boxes screaming at each other on these hot, dusty roads?'

She laughed sympathetically. 'It does seem crazy, doesn't it?'

They arrived at his office a few minutes late. As they opened the door Vicky heard phones ringing, typewriters clacking, voices talking. The building which had been so quiet and empty on her last visit was now full of people hard at work.

Ricco took her straight up to the art department on the upper floor, above the room she had seen on her previous visit. She had wondered why he hadn't shown her the art department last time, but as soon as she met the art director she knew why—Ricco wouldn't have cared to risk offending Andrea Parigi, who might have resented having his own department invaded while he wasn't on the premises.

They found him sitting in front of an easel staring fixedly at a painting.

'Andrea, sorry to interrupt, but . . .' Ricco began, but Andrea threw up a silencing hand.

*'Un momento!'* He leaned forward, peering more closely, clicking his tongue and shaking his head.

Vicky watched him curiously. A broad, stocky man, he had dark hair turning grey, a rugged face and a pair of piercing black eyes which he suddenly turned on them.

*'Si,* Ricco?'

'Andrea, this is Vicky Lloyd—you remember, I talked to you about her?'

'The English girl? Yes, of course,' He held out his hand, smiling with great warmth. *'Piacere? Lieto di fare la sua conoscenza.'*

'She doesn't speak Italian,' Ricco told him, but Vicky had by now learnt enough to realise that Andrea was merely saying hallo, nice to meet you. She answered smilingly, *'Sto bene, grazie.'*

*'Molto bene, signorina,'* said Andrea, shaking

hands with a firm, warm grip.

'Don't count on her keeping that up for long,' Ricco said drily. 'I've got an appointment, Andrea. Can I leave Vicky with you? Vicky, I'll see you at seven o'clock tonight and drive you back to the villa.'

'Thank you,' she said as he walked to the door. It closed behind him and Vicky looked at Andrea uncertainly. 'I have no experience of this sort of work, you know.'

'So, okay, what experience do you have?' He swivelled in his chair and gestured to the chair on the other side of his desk. 'Tell me about yourself. Ricco told me a little, enough for me to know you have some sort of training.'

She gave him a brief run-down on her career and years at college. 'I brought some of my work to show you, to give you an idea,' she ended, opening her bag and bringing out the sketch pad in which she had been working. 'Pastels, largely; a few watercolours—I have a large portfolio of stuff, but it's back in London and won't be sent here for a week or so.'

Andrea took the sketch pad and began to turn the pages, looking at the work with the same thoughtful eye he had been giving the picture on the easel. Vicky's gaze drifted towards that now, and Andrea said without looking up, 'What do you think of that?'

'You certainly wouldn't miss it on a display shelf.' It was a modern abstract, zigzags of flame and purple cut through by wide splashes of yellow. Vicky liked it; it was her kind of painting.

'What sort of recording would you expect to find inside that sleeve?,

'Modern, jazz or heavy rock. Maybe even pop,

depending on the group.'

Andrea grunted, his spatulate fingers closing her sketch pad. 'You like it?'

'Yes,' she replied, a little defiantly. After all, he was a Florentine; to him art would mean a certain sort of painting and sculpture, classical work, not this brash, defiant modernism.

Andrea leaned back in his chair, his fingertips together, nibbling them ruminantly. 'Do you smoke?'

'No.'

'Good. I'm trying to give up and it's driving me crazy. I couldn't cope with someone else smoking in here.' He chewed his fingertips while he stared at her; she wondered if the habit had developed since he gave up smoking.

'You know what Ricco wants? The classical series? He told you exactly what he's looking for?'

'Yes, costumes in period with the music.'

'How are you on costume?'

'I was a fashion designer—fabrics, not actual clothes, but I . . .'

'Good, good. Up your street, then? That's the phrase? Up your street?' He grinned, a gold tooth displayed. 'My wife is English, miss. She makes me speak English one day a week at home. For the children, you know? They learn while they eat, very good, yes?'

'Marvellous—I wish I was bilingual. I'm afraid my Italian is pathetic.'

He laughed. 'Okay, I teach you Italian—you correct my English when it is going haywire. You start now. Tell me—what does that mean—haywire? My wife is always using phrases I don't know.'

'I've no idea,' Vicky said blankly. 'You used it correctly in context, but I've no idea where the word comes from.'

He shrugged. 'Okay.' He went to a large cupboard and produced a printed manual. 'Read this—no need to hurry, take it home. It will give you all the technical details you will need. First, look through all the books of earlier jacket sleeves, see what we did before. And you can start studying Italian costume; we have reference books on the bookshelves at the far end of the room.,

She glanced towards them, nodding, and Andrea smiled at her. 'Okay, old chap?'

She giggled, and he eyed her enquiringly. 'That is wrong?'

'A chap is a man, not a girl,' she explained.

'Then for a girl, what?'

'Old lady, I suppose,' she said hesitatingly. 'Although it . . .'

Andrea swept aside her rider. 'Old lady, please go away and start to learn what you can. I have too much work to do, okay? We will talk tomorrow when you are finding your feet here.'

She got up. 'Thank you, Mr Parigi.'

'Andrea,' he said cheerfully. 'And my wife and I will be very happy if you come to dinner soon.'

'Thank you, I'd love to,' she said, surprised but pleased.

'Saturday?'

'Yes, that's fine with me, I'll look forward to it.'

'You can speak English with my children. I think when they grow up they will associate English with eating—at every meal they have to talk in English.'

She laughed. 'Very probably.'

'They speak better than me; when I get words

wrong, they laugh at me. Very bad children.'

And a very nice father, Vicky thought, as she settled into the far corner of the room to study her manual and a pile of books on Italian costume. She became absorbed in her work at once, and was surprised when Andrea interrupted her to suggest that it was time she went to lunch.

He took her downstairs and introduced her to some of the staff in the administrative office which she had seen on her previous visit. They took Vicky to lunch in a small family *trattoria* a short walk from the office. They had a cheap and simple meal—a typical Tuscan meal, the other girls told her. *Passatelli in brodo*, a broth made with some sort of cheese dumplings, followed by veal served with spinach and boiled potatoes and a sweet which the other girls laughingly told her was called *zuppa inglese*.

'English soup?' she repeated, puzzled, but when the dish arrived it turned out to be trifle, and the other girls laughed a great deal at her surprised expression. She couldn't eat much of it, the meal had been too filling, but it was delicious.

Vicky was ashamed to discover how many of the girls spoke some English. A few were fluent, but all of them knew some words. She was determined to learn Italian while she was living here; it would be lazy and stupid not to, so she kept asking what phrases meant, and the other girls were quite happy to teach her a few necessary expressions.

One of them was distinctly unfriendly—a thin, olive-skinned girl with brown eyes and a pointed face.

'Is it true you're living with Ricco?' she asked spitefully as they drank their coffee.

'Lina!' one of the others exclaimed, looking embarrassed.

Vicky refused to look ashamed. She calmly explained that she had an apartment in Ricco's villa, but it was quite separate. How had they found out? she wondered.

'Andrea didn't want you, you know,' Lina told her, and there was an intake of breath around the table as the girls exchanged speaking glances.

'How do you know?' Vicky asked, trying to keep her temper.

'He always gets the artwork from an agency. He doesn't need a full-time artist working for him.' Lina's dark eyes held malice. 'Ricco pushed you on to him—no wonder Andrea was so furious!'

'Oh, take no notice of her,' the other girls interjected hurriedly. 'She's a cat!'

Vicky was disturbed, though. Her instincts had been right. Ricco had manufactured this job for her, and Andrea Parigi hadn't been very happy about it.

She was relieved to find that the office staff had all left when she and Ricco set out for the villa that evening. She didn't want to walk out of the building with him while Lina watched with those sharp, malicious eyes.

He looked sideways at her curiously as they drove away. 'How did you get on with Andrea?'

'I liked him very much.'

'And the work? Found it easy?'

'Did you manufacture this job for me?' she broke out angrily.

He kept his eyes on the road, his profile cool. 'What makes you think that?'

'I picked it up—Andrea didn't really want me, did he? I'm not accusing him of saying anything, or

even giving me a hint—he was kind and pleasant—
but he doesn't usually employ full-time artists, he
commissions special work and otherwise just buys
from an art agency.'

'So?'

'So why did you offer me this job?'

'I wanted to keep you in Florence,' he said, so
casually and calmly that for a minute she didn't
quite take it in, then she flung round to stare at him
fixedly.

'Why?'

'I didn't want you to go back to London.'

'Why?' she persisted, knowing that although he
was talking with such apparent frankness he was
still being evasive.

His voice became impatient. 'Must you keep
asking questions? What difference does it make?
The job is there, you can do it—why I offered it to
you doesn't matter.'

'It matters to me,' Vicky countered tartly. 'I like
to know what I'm getting into.'

Ricco turned into the gates leading to the villa,
his tyres swishing on the gravelled drive.

'You have a suspicious little mind. There are no
strings attached, if that's what you mean.'

'That's what I mean!' she said, and Ricco shot
her an angry stare.

'You can always lock your front door at night!'

'I will, don't worry. But how many spare keys are
there?'

'You have both of them,' he said tersely. He
pulled up outside the villa and got out of the car.
Vicky clambered out the other side just in time to
find him striding round to confront her.

He grabbed her shoulders and shook her furiously. 'If I wanted a woman I wouldn't have to buy myself one—with a job or anything else!'

'Don't manhandle me!' Vicky snapped, jerking away. 'Bianca Fancelli may like rough stuff, but I don't!'

His face altered, the dark blue eyes glittering with mockery. 'You seem obsessed with Bianca!'

Vicky's face burnt. She hadn't meant to say that, it had just slipped out.

'If anyone's obsessed with her, it's you, not me,' she said furiously, turning on her heel. She remembered the glassy floor, and slowed down once she was inside the long gallery. Every time she walked down the vaulted garden-like room she felt surprised by the strangeness of being here, living in a place as extraordinary and beautiful as this one.

Ricco loomed up behind her as she put her key into the ancient lock. 'Just because some man treated you badly, there's no need to slap me down all the time,' he said harshly.

Ricco was like this incredible gallery—he surprised and riveted your attention, but he was also dangerous if you let yourself walk unwarily. One false step, and your feet would slide from under you.

She opened her door and was about to walk into the apartment, when he caught her waist, his hand firm and inexorable.

'I'm talking to you!'

'Really? I thought you were shouting,' She tried to pull away, but his hand gripped her more tightly.

'Was he much older than you? A married man, you said—a father figure, was he? Your own father died years ago, I gather. You must have been very young at the time. It probably had a traumatic effect on you, left you vulnerable to older men . . .'

'What absolute rubbish,' Vicky snarled, turning on him. 'Don't you try to analyse me! That cuts both ways, you know. What are *you* looking for in a woman? Didn't you say your mother was dead? Well, I suppose that would explain why you're so fascinated by Bianca!'

He stared down at her, apparently stupefied, then began to laugh. 'You wicked little cat! Bianca's years younger than I am.'

She opened her eyes wide at him. 'I'd never have guessed! And before you start casting yourself in the role of my next father figure, I am definitely not into older men!'

She pulled herself away while he was taking that in and managed to slam the door, leaving him on the other side.

She was very tired that evening and went to bed early again. An owl hooted somewhere in the gardens just as she was drifting off to sleep, and she got up to close the shutters over her bedroom windows to shut out the mournful cry. It was a very dark night, but as she was reaching up to fasten the shutters she caught a tiny red glow in the darkness, and then the scent of a cigar. Vicky stood there, hearing a slow footstep on the gravel path, the grate of a heel. Ricco was walking in the garden, smoking a cigar. His face was a pale blur between the leaves of a lilac tree and she stared towards it, wondering why he wasn't asleep. He had to get up early too.

He took another step, and at that instant glanced towards her window. She knew he had seen her, for he turned that way, the cigar in his hand making a small red arc as he gestured.

'Can't you sleep either?' He walked over to the window and stood on the other side of the glass, staring at her.

It was a cool spring night, a little wind stirring the branches in the garden, but suddenly Vicky was hot; she felt beads of sweat break out on her temples, and her legs turned to rubber.

Without a word she hurriedly pulled the shutters together and bolted them, almost running to bed to climb in under the sheet. She was shaking. Under Ricco's stare she had become conscious of wearing a short, thin nightshirt of fine cotton which hid very little of her body. There had been glass between them, yet his eyes had had an impact almost as violent as if he had been touching her instead of merely staring.

She curled up and tried to get to sleep; it wasn't easy. Next morning when Ricco picked her up she felt tense and uneasy long before he tapped on the door. Living here, so close to him, was going to be more of a problem than she had feared. She had told herself that she could handle him—she hadn't reckoned with having to handle her own instincts too.

Ricco gave her a dry look when she opened the door. 'Speaking to me today?'

'Of course,' she said as coolly as she could.

'Well, that's nice,' he said. 'If it bothers you to have me looking at you when you're only wearing your nightdress, you'd better not stand at the window like that in future.'

'Oh, shut up!' snapped Vicky, getting into his car.

She saw very little of him over the next few days, except in the morning and evening when he drove her to and from the office. She was totally occupied in what she was doing in the art department, and time seemed to flash past. To her relief she found

Andrea very helpful; whenever he had time he would give her tips on how to conceive ideas for the jackets, show her earlier artwork, discuss why he had picked it and how successful it had been. Vicky felt she was learning all the time, and by the end of the week she was much more hopeful about being able to do this job.

On the Friday afternoon she was alone in the art department when Ricco walked into the room. She looked up, startled, her eyes immediately wary.

'Andrea isn't here.'

'I didn't want Andrea, I wanted you.'

Her eyes flickered at the phrasing and his mouth twitched impatiently.

'That wasn't a double meaning.'

'I didn't think it was!'

'No? You looked as if you did.'

'Oh, really, stop picking me up on everything I say and do!' she burst out, and Ricco put a finger on her lips to silence her, his face quizzical. He smiled, and Vicky muttered, 'Sorry I got mad.'

As her lips moved under his finger, the words breathed out on his skin, Ricco bent towards her. Vicky froze, her eyes restlessly skating over his face. She didn't want to feel that stab of sharp attraction, but she couldn't deny, even to herself, that she did feel it.

'Did Andrea tell you that he's invited me to dinner this Saturday too?' he murmured, staring at her mouth and still tracing the curve of it with that long index finger.

'No,' she said breathlessly, mind racing. Andrea had invited him to make up the party? Why would he do that unless he believed that she and Ricco were intimately involved? Andrea knew by now

that she was living in Ricco's house; no doubt he
had drawn his own conclusions, and Vicky flushed
deeper at the realisation of what that would mean.
Andrea was sophisticated and knew Ricco very
well. Had other women lived in the villa before her?
Susan hadn't mentioned that she wasn't the first,
but then Susan might not have known, or might be
reluctant to repeat gossip of that sort.

'We're supposed to be there by eight—I'll drive
you there. He lives on the outskirts of the city. It's
going to take us half an hour, so we'll leave at seven-
thirty.'

They were so absorbed in each other that they
hadn't noticed the click of the door opening, but
they both heard the sharp intake of breath and the
tap-tap of heels on the floor. Vicky's nostrils
quivered at the powerful scent of a woman's
perfume as she turned her head to stare at Bianca
Fancelli.

The high-pitched spate of Italian made no sense
to her, of course, but she didn't need a translation.
Bianca's rage vibrated in her voice, her black eyes
burned, darting from Vicky's flushed face to
Ricco's wary one. At every stabbing word she
gestured, a rolled-up magazine clutched in one
hand. Vicky got the feeling that at any minute
Bianca might beat Ricco over the head with it, but
Bianca suddenly threw it on to the desk, dropped
her purse next to it, unbuttoned the short fantailed
white mink she was wearing and stalked close to
Ricco, continuing her monologue eye to eye with
him, ignoring Vicky.

Vicky would have left the room if she could have
got up and exited without attracting Bianca's
unwanted attention. She lowered her eyes and kept

very still, letting Ricco cope with his lady-friend.

The magazine Bianca had flung down was slowly unrolling; Vicky watched it absently from the corner of her eye.

With a wild shock of disbelief she saw her own face appear, a photograph in colour, blown up too large, a distorted image she only just recognised. Her head swung quickly and she looked up at Ricco, eyes wide in alarm.

What was Bianca saying to him? Had she recognised Vicky on the cover of the magazine? Was she telling Ricco that he was now employing Miller Osborne's missing fiancée?

Ricco must have sensed the sharp movement, and he slid a sideways glance at her. Hurriedly she looked down, her face burning.

Bianca stopped, mid-spate, flung round to glare at Vicky and spat out two words that made Vicky stiffen with affront. She was pretty sure she knew what that meant, and she didn't like the job description.

'*Zitta!*' snapped Ricco, and that, too, Vicky understood. Be quiet, he had said, in a tone that Bianca did not like at all.

Grabbing her purse, Bianca made for the door. Vicky picked up the magazine as Ricco followed the other woman; she was about to drop it into the wastepaper basket when Bianca stalked back and snatched it away from her. The cover ripped— Vicky had been holding the magazine too tightly. Bianca made noises like a kettle boiling. She waved the magazine at Vicky, pouring out more Italian, then her eyes narrowed and she stopped talking to stare, closely, frowningly.

Vicky somehow held her stare, but she was very

cold and pale. Bianca looked down at the photograph on the cover, looked at Vicky again, staring at her short blonde hair. The girl on the cover had dark hair, of course, smooth and straight, brushed down over her shoulders. That made the face seem thinner, and Vicky's make-up had been different.

'*Come si chiama Lei?*' demanded Bianca.

Vicky knew perfectly well that the other woman was asking her name, but she didn't admit she understood, she simply gave a blank shrug.

'*Bianca, che cosa c'è, ora?*'

Ricco's voice from the door made Bianca turn her head, the sloe-black eyes intent, a spark of malice in them—or was that Vicky's imagination? Nervously she tried to read the other woman's face. Had she recognised her? Or had she merely picked up a resemblance, a similarity, and begun to wonder?

Giving Vicky one last hostile look, Bianca walked towards the door, taking the magazine with her, clenched in her hand again. Vicky heard the sound of the footsteps receding down the stairs. She collapsed into a chair with her hands over her face.

What had the article in the magazine been about? She wished she read Italian, but the splash headline on the cover had made no sense to her. All she had picked out was her own name and Miller's, his in much larger type, coming first.

She must somehow get hold of a copy of the magazine and ask Susan to translate it for her. She wished she had noted what it was called, but in her anxiety over seeing her own face on the cover she hadn't thought of looking at the name of the magazine.

Had Bianca recognised her? If she had, would she tell Ricco? Vicky began to wish she had told

him herself. She should have warned him about the
sort of publicity that might blow up in her face if
Miller and Sunny ever found out where she was, but
when they first met she had been desperate not to be
recognised, and by the time she knew him and was
pretty sure he would never betray her it had been
too late. She had been unwilling to talk about Miller
to him. She had been unwilling to talk about Miller
to anyone. The whole subject made her sick. It had
been such a revelation to her of the depths of
corruption which existed; she had been so naïve
and blind until she walked into that spider's web.
She had escaped, but she knew she would never be
the same again, and she hated talking about it.

Ricco wasn't going to like it when he found out
how much she had lied to him. He had been angry
enough when he discovered that she had lied about
her name, but this was much worse.

It was only then she admitted how much it
mattered to her what Ricco thought, and the
admission shook her. In a few weeks he had become
important; she didn't know how she could have
been so stupid as to let another good-looking man
get to her like that, but it was too late to re-erect her
shattered barriers. Ricco had got through them.

# CHAPTER EIGHT

VICKY spent the Saturday morning shopping with Susan and had lunch with her cousin and David in their villa. They were intrigued to discover that she was having dinner with Ricco. David teased her about it; Susan was faintly worried.

'I can handle him,' Vicky assured her, with a confidence she was far from feeling. 'And anyway, we're having dinner with the Parigi family—with children to chaperon us, Ricco hasn't a chance of trying anything.'

'During dinner, maybe not, but what about later, when you're driving back alone?' David teased. 'In the moonlight, by the river? Very romantic! That Lamborghini has a sex appeal that turns girls' heads.'

'Which is more than its owner does,' retorted Vicky, and got an incredulous look from Susan, who clearly didn't believe that. Nor did David, who hooted derisively.

'Go on! You know you fancy him.'

'I'm not arguing with you any more,' Vicky said with dignity. 'Can I have some more coffee, Susan?'

'You do like the job, though, don't you?' Susan asked as she refilled Vicky's cup.

'It's fascinating—next week Andrea may be taking me to watch a recording session in the studios.'

'Have you come up with any ideas for a cover yet?' David asked, relaxing in a chair with a sigh.

'Not yet,' said Vicky, uncertainty in her eyes. She now had a pretty good idea of the techniques involved—what was required was inspiration, and so far that hadn't struck. 'It'll come,' she said, whistling in the dark. At least, she hoped it would.

That evening she had a hard time trying to make up her mind what to wear. Her own uncertainty irritated her to the point where she felt like screaming. She was only going to dinner with a pleasant family—it wasn't a world-shaking event. Why was she so screwed up about it?

What if Ricco was taking her? Was that any reason for dithering about like an idiot? She firmly took down a dress made from a fabric she had designed herself, a warm rose-red printed with faint white spirals that looked from a distance like tiny roses. It had been designed for her by a friend from art college who had helped her to sew it. It had a tight waist, a full skirt that swirled as she moved and a delicate lace collar on a low, round neckline.

Every time Vicky wore it she had poignant memories of her last year at college. Her best friend had planned to join a good fashion house and from there launch into designing for herself, but she had married and become pregnant, so her career had gone out of the window as soon as she left college. Vicky had occasionally heard from her since—they had always talked of starting up in business together. Vicky would design fabrics, Annie would design the clothes. They would be famous and make their fortune.

It hadn't turned out like that. Fate had taken a hand. Vicky made a face, sighing. It would have been fun.

Ricco arrived promptly and leaned on her front

door, looking her up and down, whistling.

She flushed. 'Thank you.' She ran her eyes over him in deliberate imitation and whistled back. He deserved it, casual in pale blue cotton slacks and a blue-and-white shirt, a cotton jacket matching the slacks over that. The fashion was Italian, striking, very elegant. Vicky loved the flowing lines and cool colours.

His eyes mocked. 'Am I supposed to be taken aback? I'm glad you approve.'

She looked into the dark blue eyes, smiling. Bianca hadn't said anything to him, she was sure of that. It made her feel relaxed, happy. Her smile seemed to run through her whole body.

'A pity we're not going dancing,' said Ricco, watching her lock her door. 'That dress was meant to be danced in—maybe on the way back from Andrea's, if it isn't too late, we might stop somewhere?'

They emerged into the soft dusk of an Italian evening, the air heavy with scents of late spring. Ricco unlocked his car and watched her slide into it, then walked round to join her. Vicky was silent, her head cloudy with a languor she couldn't explain, watching him through her lashes, her head back against the seat, her pulses beating slowly and sleepily. She didn't feel like having dinner with strangers, making polite small talk. Ricco was right—it was a night for dancing. She wondered what it would feel like, being held in his arms, moving with him to music. Her pulses picked up and beat faster.

'Music?' He turned on a tape player and a guitar began throbbing; gypsy music, Spanish, she thought vaguely.

'One of yours?'

'Of course.' He turned his head, smiling, his teeth a white flash against brown skin. 'Andrea suggests you might like to sit in at the studio one day next week. I'll fix it.'

'Thank you.' The deep passionate beat of the music sounded inside her, in her bloodstream, in her body.

The city was crammed with traffic, as usual, those narrow streets hot and stuffy with petrol fumes and noisy with the sound of engines roaring. Ricco drove without speaking, his tanned hands resting on the wheel, his body poised patiently, and she watched him drowsily, beginning to admit that she wanted to touch him, to trace the hard contours of that face, learn the feel of his body under her hands. The gypsy music beat higher, she could hardly breathe.

Ricco turned into a less busy road and picked up speed. He shot her a look that gleamed with awareness, and her eyes quickly dropped. He knew she had been staring; had he picked up what she was feeling?

Oh, God, I hope not, she thought, very hot. A moment later he had parked and shut off the music, and Vicky stumbled out of the car without waiting for him to move first.

It was a pleasant evening, after all. Andrea's wife, Lucy, was a calm, friendly woman at least ten years older than Vicky, perhaps more. Their children were lively and easy with adults, used to having grown-up conversations, interested in what went on around the table, able to enter into discussions about music and books and television. The food was very good; Lucy had made a fruit cocktail to start with, and then served a dish of green and white tagliatelle with a meat sauce which was quite delicious. 'Straw and hay,' Lucy told her when Vicky asked what the dish was called.

The children laughed. Vicky looked at them, glanced at Ricco.

'No, really? What is it called?'

*'Paglia e fieno,'* said Ricco, grinning.

'And what does that mean?'

'Straw and hay,' they all chorused, laughing, and when she refused to believe them Lucy went off to find a dictionary and proved that they weren't making it up.

Lucy didn't look particularly English, her skin was so brown and her eyes were even darker. At a glance she would certainly pass for an Italian, but her accent betrayed her when she opened her mouth, and she had curly brown hair with a streak of red in it.

She and Vicky washed up together after the meal. Vicky had to insist; she wanted a chance to get to know Lucy better without the men around. As they worked she told Lucy about Susan and David.

'Susan's made some friends, with the wives of men who work with David, but her Italian isn't very good yet and she feels a bit lonely here. That's partly why I'm staying on—I know Susan likes having me near her.'

'It isn't easy, when you first move to Italy, but once you can speak the language it gets easier. You have to make the effort to find friends, but that applies anywhere. If you moved to a strange town in England you'd have the same problem.'

'I'm planning to have a small housewarming party soon—mostly people from the office. I hope you'll come. I'd like you to meet Susan.'

'I'd love to,' said Lucy, putting away plates in a wall cupboard. 'Andrea tells me you're living in part of Ricco's house.' She glanced round. 'The empty wing, isn't it?'

'That's right,' Vicky said guardedly, wondering what Lucy thought of that.

'I like Ricco, he's been very good to us. When my eldest boy, Piero, was knocked down by a car Ricco insisted on paying for a specialist from Milan, the best man in the country. I think if he hadn't done that Piero might have lost his sight. He had to have a very difficult operation immediately. Even a delay of a few days might have meant his chances were remote, but thanks to Ricco the operation was performed almost at once and was a hundred per cent successful. I'll never be able to forget what he did for us. Neither will Andrea.' Lucy turned, wiping her hands on a tea towel. 'He's a nice man.' She smiled. 'Far too nice to get caught by someone like Bianca Fancelli!'

Vicky carefully put down the coffee cup she was drying. 'You think he may marry her?' she asked, hoping she sounded casual.

Lucy grimaced. 'I hope not.'

Vicky's stomach was clenched as if someone had just hit her there. She listened as Lucy talked, trying to look calm.

'Bianca's a singer—first and last a singer! Everything else in her life has to fit her work, she doesn't care twopence for anyone but Bianca Fancelli and her career.' Lucy's face was ironic. 'If she does marry Ricco it will be because he's useful to her, and she'll give him hell. She's ruthless, spoilt, selfish—a typical star.'

Vicky felt a cold jab of comprehension, recognising the description—Bianca and Miller were two of a kind, their careers were what mattered, and the people who got involved with them were unimportant and expendable. Their amorality was instinctive, a defence against the many people who tried to use them. They made sure that they were the users, and in a way that was understandable, but it made them poor risks for anyone stupid enough to love them.

'Do you think he's in love with her?' she asked huskily, and Lucy shot her an odd look.

'I wouldn't like to guess—Ricco plays his cards close to his chest, but he has seen a lot of her over the past couple of years, although he couldn't really avoid doing so considering she's such a major recording star.'

'She's good, isn't she?' said Vicky, grimly determined to face facts.

'Good?' Lucy looked at her drily. 'She's fabulous, and she knows it.'

'Does Andrea talk about his work much?'

'Endlessly.'

'Do you go to the opera often?'

'Whenever we can get a baby-sitter. We have all our favourite operas on disc, but however good the recording it can't compare with a stage performance, that's a feast for the eye as well as the ear, and the singers get more of a buzz from having an audience, their performances are often better. Bianca, in particular, comes over the footlights like a typhoon. She has tremendous stage presence; when she's on, even if she has her mouth shut, you can't take your eyes off her.'

Vicky's teeth set like concrete; she went on

smiling, but it hurt. Why should she imagine that Ricco was interested in her when Bianca had ten times her sex appeal, plus all that talent, beauty, sheer knockout presence? She should have remembered her first impression of him—like Miller, he was a flirt.

Lucy opened the kitchen window wider. The dark night sky was cloudy, the air heavy and humid. 'I've got a hunch it may rain overnight. We haven't had any rain for days, so it will do the gardens good.' She turned, smiling. 'Shall we see what the men are up to?'

The children were in bed and asleep by now. The men were talking shop, but when Lucy and Vicky came in Ricco got up, stretching his long body with a smothered yawn.

'I'm afraid we must be going, Lucy. I think a storm is on the way, don't you? I'd like to get home before it breaks. Thanks for a wonderful evening.'

Vicky added her own thanks. 'And don't forget my party—I'll let Andrea know when I've fixed the date.'

Andrea and his wife waved goodbye from their door, their arms around each other. Vicky looked back, waving. 'I like them very much,' she said to Ricco.

'So do I.' He threw her a smile. 'And what was all that about a party?'

'A housewarming, it seemed a good idea.' She made a mock face at him. 'I'd forgotten you were my landlord—do I need permission?'

'Am I invited?'

'Is that the price of permission?' She laughed. 'Yes, of course you are.'

'Then I agree, a housewarming is a good idea.'

The streets were far less empty now, and they drove back faster than they had come.

'Who else are you asking?' he queried.

'Some of the girls from the office—if that's okay with you?'

'Why ask me? You're the one giving the party.'

Vicky watched him through her lashes; his face seemed abstracted, brooding.

'You're welcome to bring someone,' she said huskily. 'Bianca.' She stopped short as his head swung towards her, his dark blue eyes intent. 'Or anyone you like,' she added hurriedly under that probing stare. The last thing she wanted was to have Bianca Fancelli at her party, in her apartment, in the same room with her; especially if Ricco was there too, and she had to watch them together. It had been bad enough the other night, seeing them up there on the loggia, knowing that they were going out to dinner, might well come back to Ricco's villa afterwards and make love. It would be ten times worse if they were in the same room, but she had made herself suggest that he brought Bianca. Perhaps she was a masochist, she thought, but her only way of dealing with those sharp stabs of jealousy was to grit her teeth and pretend she didn't care.

His face had an odd, ironic cast in the stormy light. 'You want me to bring Bianca to your party?'

'If you want to,' she muttered through clenched teeth.

'But you don't mind if I do?' Ricco enquired.

She made an acquiescing noise. She couldn't actually speak.

His expression was bland. 'You're very tolerant—after what she callled you yesterday!'

Vicky went red. 'You know I don't speak Italian very well.'

'You didn't understand? Well, it was a very colloquial phrase—shall I translate?'

'No, thank you!' she said furiously. 'I got the general drift from the way she said it.'

'I suspected you had,' he drawled, amused. 'Bianca doesn't much care for you, it seems.'

'What have I ever done to her? Until yesterday she has always pretended I didn't exist.'

'You have a very convenient memory,' he murmured, and she looked quickly at his profile. He was watching the road as he drove and smiling to himself. Vicky did not like that smile; it held far too much complacency.

'What does that mean?' she asked.

'You've apparently forgotten that when Bianca walked into the office she found us having what she felt was a very intimate conversation.'

Vicky stiffened. Had it given his ego a boost to know that he had made Bianca jealous? Was that why he was paying her so much attention? She was so furious she felt like hitting him.

'Well, she needn't be jealous of me,' she snapped. 'Because I'm not in the least interested in you!' After that there was a long silence between them as Ricco drove with his foot down, frowning. As they turned into the lion-topped gates, Vicky threw a look towards her cousin's house and saw that the windows were all dark. Susan and David must be in bed now; it was gone eleven. She yawned. She felt very tired herself.

'Well, we beat the storm,' said Ricco as he parked in the garage at the back of the house. They walked round to the main entrance and said goodnight by

Vicky's private entrance.

'See you at crack of dawn,' Ricco teased as she let herself in, and she made a face at him over her shoulder.

She had just undressed when all the lights went off. For a moment she just froze there, in the darkness, startled, then she saw the night split with a silver flash and ten seconds later there was a deafening crash of thunder. The storm had arrived and, it appeared, knocked out the electricity supply. Ricco had warned her that that sometimes happened. The wiring in the house wasn't all it might be. She groped blindly for a dressing-gown, hoping fervently that Ricco had a lightning conductor on the roof of the house. The storm was raging violently just overhead, and she kept starting as lightning crashed downwards outside followed almost at once by peals of thunder.

Vicky couldn't remember ever being through a storm like it. The noise was deafening, the flashes of lightning made her eyes hurt.

She almost didn't hear the knocking on her outer door, through the clashing of thunder, but at last she realised that Ricco was checking that she was okay. Still shaky with nerves, she groped her way to the door and opened it. Ricco stood there with a flashlight. He shone it on her face and she blinked, putting up a hand.

'Hey, I can't see a thing with that shining right into my eyes!'

'Have you got any candles?'

'No, have you?'

'Yes, plenty—I brought some round for you—the power may not be restored for quite a while.' He had lowered the flashlight's beam and now she

could see him. He had undressed, too; she saw his
bare legs below the edge of a black towelling
bathrobe.

'I was in the bath,' he said drily. 'I almost cracked
my skull open, slipping on the soap when I stood up
as the lights went out.' He raised the flashlight a
little; she saw his face and gave an exclamation of
concern.

'Your forehead's bleeding—I think you did hit
your head.' She leaned forward to see the cut better.
'You'd better come in and let me put a plaster on
that.'

He came inside, shutting the door, and they went
to the bathroom. Vicky found some cotton wool,
moistened it and cleaned the small cut. It wasn't as
bad as it had looked at first, more blood than
wound. She gently dried it, very conscious now of
Ricco's nearness, her mouth suddenly dry as she
touched his skin. He had put down the flashlight
and was perching on the edge of the vast bath.
Vicky was standing close to him, too close, she felt,
sensing his eyes on the deep lapels of her dressing-
gown.

Could he see that she had nothing on beneath it?
Her fingers trembled as she applied the small
plaster, pressing it down over the cut.

'There,' she said huskily, trying to step back.
Ricco's hand snaked round her waist and held her.
His other hand cupped the nape of her neck before
she could break away, pulling her head down.
'Thanks,' he whispered just before he kissed her,
ignoring the resistance of her tense body.

Vicky tried to resist that kiss, but his mouth softly
teased with a sensuous, lazy movement until her lips
parted. For a moment they kissed, her eyes shut but

aware of the flash of lightning outside—or was that
wild white light part of her own reaction to Ricco's
caress?

She mustn't let things get out of hand, she thought
dazedly, putting her hands up to push him away.
Her palms flattened on his wide shoulders, then one
slid helplessly, of its own volition, and she felt his
warm skin as she gripped the side of his throat.

'Let go, please,' she muttered, struggling. She
should never have invited him into the flat; what
had she let loose now?

He suddenly pulled her downwards across his lap,
her head cradled on his shoulder and her feet right
off the ground, and without taking his mouth from
hers coolly slid one hand inside her dressing gown .
If he hadn't guessed that she was naked underneath
it, he knew now. His mouth was still for a second—
in surprise?

Before she could lift her head to demand that he
let go of her, the kiss deepened, his tongue warm
and intrusive, but it wasn't his mouth that was
worrying her now, it was what his hands were
doing. Their slow, seductive caress made her head
swim. She knew she had to do something at once,
before it was too late, so she struggled to get up with
a frightened violence that sent them both tumbling
backwards.

Vicky gave a cry of shock as she realised they
were falling, and the next second they landed with a
thud in the deep bath. She lay sprawled across
Ricco, who wasn't moving. Vicky breathlessly tried
to scramble up, only to come against the rigid bar of
his arm across her back. Lightning split the sky
again, showing her his face, the eyes wide open,
showing her his body also, the dark robe thrown

open in the fall. Ricco was naked too, and he was
staring at her, breathing thickly. Arched back as far
as his arm would permit her, her breasts pale in the
darkness, her thighs tangled with his, she stared
down at him, trembling.

For a space of time the sexual tension between
them dragged like a taut wire, and then Ricco
deliberately broke it.

His voice husky, he said, 'Now I've got a bang on
the other side of my head. This is obviously one of
those nights!'

Vicky felt his arm fall and knew she was free to
get up. Her scramble out of the bath was undigni-
fied. With trembling fingers she retied her belt as
Ricco stepped out of the bath too.

Vicky looked shyly at him. His face was full of
amusement, and suddenly she began to laugh
wildly, staggering across the room. The laughter
was a release and it was safer. She had never in her
life felt such powerful electric tension between
herself and a man. Her body still ached with a desire
she hadn't expected, her breasts were hot and heavy
with it.

'I'd better go before I collect any more cuts and
bruises,' Ricco said drily, moving to the door as he
tied his belt. 'You're a lethal lady in a bathroom!
Remind me never to kiss you when there's a bath
around for you to hit me with.'

She followed him to the door, still shuddering
with laughter. He held his flashlight down, making
yellow circles on the stone floor. He had given her a
pile of candles which she clutched in her hand, but
they needed neither flashlight nor candles to see by
while the storm raged overhead, a new flash of

lightning ripping through the sky every moment or so.

'Good night,' he said, his eyes gleaming at her as he turned to walk away, and she watched him for a second or two before she shut the door. She only had to call him back and he would stay. Her senses cried out for the satisfaction they had begun to expect, but Vicky firmly closed the door and leaned her hot face on it. She didn't know how she was going to be able to walk back to her bedroom.

And how was she going to face Ricco tomorrow morning? Then as she tumbled into bed she remembered—tomorrow was Sunday, she wouldn't have to get up at crack of dawn, neither would Ricco. It was almost one by the time she got to sleep, torn between wishing she hadn't sent him away and feeling glad that she hadn't given in to those crazy impulses.

When she woke up in the morning, the storm had blown itself out and the air was calm and still in the sunlit gardens, but her own emotional storm hadn't quietened down in the same way. She thought of Ricco the instant she opened her eyes and groaned, hurriedly shutting them again.

That didn't make the memory of last night disappear. It brooded over her as she lay in bed listening to the call of the birds in the garden. She had told him angrily as they drove back from Andrea's house that she wasn't in the least interested in him. Just an hour later she had been in his arms, lost to all common sense, making it very clear that she was violently attracted to him.

No wonder he had smiled with that maddening complacency last night! She had made a fool of herself.

She spent that Sunday quietly with Susan and David, driving through the Tuscany hills, watching the misty blue lights of further hills recede and advance, looking back towards the Arno valley to see the green fields, olive groves, orchards and swathes of pine and evergreen trees.

When they got back it was dusk, and the lights were on in the big villa. She let herself into her own apartment without running into Ricco. Was he alone? she wondered. Or was Bianca there again tonight? If he was playing out some strategic game, using Vicky to make Bianca jealous, he was obviously succeeding. There had been no doubt about her jealousy on Friday in the art department—she had raged like a tiger snapping at prey which is out of reach.

Vicky stayed awake for hours brooding over being used in that ruthless fashion. When would she start believing her own first instincts? Ricco wasn't in the film world, but his business dealt in the same debased coin. This was just another part of the same jungle; the animals were all as sharp in tooth and claw and as hungry for prey. She had picked that up the minute she met him, but she kept forgetting. Ricco made her forget, with his mocking, intimate smiles and those seductive hands. When he began to kiss her, her rational self had flown out of the window; the submerged desire she didn't want to give in to had taken over and she had lost her head.

From now on she was going to keep him at a distance, he wasn't getting another chance to do that to her.

# CHAPTER NINE

WHEN she joined Ricco next morning his eyes were
bright and intimate, but one look at her face and his
expression changed.

'What's wrong?'

'Nothing. Why should anything be wrong?'
Vicky walked on with a fixed smile. It felt as though
her teeth were set in concrete, but her pride
demanded that she shouldn't let him think she was
vulnerable to him. She had to look cheerful at all
costs.

As they drove out of the gates Susan was cleaning
the upper windows of her house; she waved and
Vicky waved back.

'How is Susan?' asked Ricco. 'I haven't seen her
for a few days. Everything okay now between her
and David?'

'Back to normal, thank God.'

'Thanks to me, don't you mean?' he said
teasingly.

'Oh, you confuse yourself with the deity, do you?'

'I thought you might,' he murmured, watching
her averted face quizzically. 'You seem very sharp
this morning. Did you have a bad night?'

She shrugged. 'I've had better.'

'What was keeping you awake? Or should I ask
who?'

She violently objected to the light, teasing
manner. He was so pleased with himself; he really
thought he had her fooled. She felt the vicious

instincts of someone with a pin eying a balloon they are about to puncture.

'It wasn't you,' she snapped. 'You'll never keep me awake.'

He took his eyes off the road to stare in maddening surprise. 'You *are* bad-tempered this morning!'

'Are you trying to drive into the back of that lorry?' Vicky asked, checking that her seatbelt was clipped in case he actually did crash into something.

He paid more attention to his driving for a few moments, then said quietly, 'Do you ever think about the guy you left behind in England?'

'As rarely as possible!'

'He must have hit you badly to make you this angry.' She felt him watching her sideways again as they drew up at some traffic lights.

'It isn't him I get angry about,' Vicky said tensely. 'It's my own stupidity for ever falling for him in the first place.'

He put out his hand and patted one of hers. 'We all make mistakes, Vicky. We just have to learn from them, and then forget them.'

She gave him a cynical smile. 'That's exactly what I plan to do.'

'All men aren't like him!'

'I didn't say *all* men are.'

He watched her, frowning. 'I'm not, for a start.'

'No?'

'No!' he insisted, starting to sound irritated. 'Look, I resent being classed with a man like that. I'm trying to be patient with you . . .'

'How gracious of you, remind me to feel grateful.' She bitterly resented his condescending tone. Who did he think he was, being patient with her? What mountain did he think he lived on?

'Maybe it's the time of the month,' he began through his teeth.

'Leave my anatomy out of this!'

'Don't you mean biology?' Ricco snarled.

'To you, I wouldn't use the word—it immediately makes you think of sex, but then every word in the dictionary seems to make you think of sex.'

It wasn't until he had pulled up outside the office that he turned a normal colour again. Before she got out of the Lamborghini he clamped an angrily detaining hand on her arm, turning on her with bared teeth.

'If I had a suspicious mind, I'd wonder if you're so angry because I didn't stay on Saturday night,' he said icily.

She would have hit him if he wasn't grasping her right hand. Instead she said a word in Italian which she had sometimes heard Andrea say when he was in a temper.

The effect on Ricco was electrifying. He looked at her as if he couldn't believe his ears. Vicky took the opportunity to escape while he was still reeling. As she ran up the stairs to the art department she wondered what the word meant, and decided it might be wiser not to ask Andrea.

She was in an irritable, edgy mood all morning, but after a good lunch and some local wine she felt faintly ashamed of her bad temper. Ricco couldn't realise it, but most of her anger had been aimed at herself for making the same mistake twice. She had known he would be dangerous to her peace of mind the minute she set eyes on him. He attracted her the way nectar attracts humming birds. She'd told herself she wouldn't let him matter, but her willpower was practically nil. On Saturday it had vanished altogether. He was right—she was in a temper because if he *had* decided to stay all night she wouldn't have tried to stop him.

She imagined he'd keep out of her way for the rest of the day, but to her surprise he showed up in the art department that afternoon, eying her frowningly.

'Want to come to the studio to watch a recording session?'

'*Bene,*' Andrea said at once, nodding vehemently. 'Go, go, Vicky. You will learn a lot about the business and I will get some peace and quiet.' He grinned at Ricco. 'She is being a bear with a sore head today—I don't know why. Maybe it's love, love makes you bad-tempered.'

Vicky was cross and pink. 'Don't be silly,' she muttered, collecting her handbag while the two men watched, their expressions amused.

'It couldn't be love,' Ricco told Andrea mockingly. 'Her heart's impervious.'

'I don't believe it,' Andrea denied, shaking his head. 'A nice girl like her!'

'Cold, though,' Ricco murmured, watching her walk towards the door. 'Cold as the Alps in winter.'

'But even ice thaws,' Andrea reminded him. 'A little sunshine, a little fire.'

'Any man brave enough would need a blowtorch to melt that ice,' Ricco shrugged.

'Oh, do stop it!' snapped Vicky, turning on them. 'If you two have had enough fun, can we get going? At this rate, by the time we get to the studio they'll have finished recording and gone home.'

Ricco drove them the half-mile to a narrow back street in a less busy part of Florence. As he parked he gave Vicky a wry look.

'Got it out of your system yet?'

She grimaced. 'Sorry I was edgy.'

'We all get days like that,' he said, and she looked up to find him smiling at her in a way that made her heart turn over.

'I wish I didn't like you so much,' she said before she could stop herself, and Ricco's brows rose, his blue eyes laughing.

'Is that a backhanded compliment?'

'More of a heartfelt prayer,' she said, getting out of the car.

The studio was in a draughty old building which reminded Vicky of a barn. The studio itself had a strange, lunar atmosphere because of the sound-proofing of the high walls. There were no windows, the walls were padded with quilted polystyrene tiles which were vaguely like thick eggboxes, the ceiling was similarly soundproofed, and the floors were tiled with rubber so that footsteps made no noise.

Ricco pulled open a heavy swing door with a porthole in the centre of it and waved Vicky through. She found herself in a brilliantly lit little room; two men wearing headphones sat at a bank of electrical equipment in front of a glass wall. They turned to stare at her, frowning, then recognised Ricco as he came in behind her, letting the heavy door swing shut softly.

'*Ciao,*' they said, smiling.

Vicky saw that below them lay a large rectangular studio. There were several high mikes set up in front of stools on which sat some young men with guitars propped between their knees and cups of coffee in their hands.

'Coffee break?' Ricco asked drily, and one of the

engineers took off his headphones and swivelled in his chair to nod.

'This is Vicky Lloyd, she's working in our art department now,' said Ricco, and the man leaned over to shake hands. 'Vicky, this is Giorgio, our best sound engineer. He's been with me since I set up the studio.'

Giorgio was in his fifties, heavily built with receding hair and piercing black eyes. His tan seemed to be permanent; she had the feeling he was always this deep, dark brown.

'Hi, Vicky,' he said, and again she thought how stupid it was that she shouldn't speak their language, while they all seemed so fluent in hers. 'You've come to sit in on a session, Ricco tells me. Pull up a chair.'

'You all speak such good English,' she said, and he smiled.

'We need to—we record so many American and English artists.'

Ricco drew a chair over to the bank of instruments and Vicky sat down, murmuring, 'Thanks.' Ricco took a chair on her left. Giorgio was on her right, and he began explaining the layout of his instruments.

The young men in the studio were laughing and playing the fool, throwing their empty coffee cups at each other.

'High spirits,' Ricco said drily. 'Is it going well, Giorgio?'

Giorgio looked at his watch. 'Five minutes, and we'll try for a recording. They've been rehearsing for a couple of hours while we juggle with the electronics.' He glanced at Vicky sideways. 'I have quite an array here—an orchestra at my fingertips.'

He ran his hand lightly over the equipment. 'Electronic drums, keyboard, woodwind section, echo chamber—I can make any sound you want just by pressing one of these switches.'

'Modern recording equipment practically does away with the need for live musicians,' Ricco said drily. 'Of course, the musicians' union would kick up murder if we tried to do that, and I wouldn't want to, anyway. Electronic music can't replace the live musician in my book, but it certainly helps with the cost of recordings and the time spent in the studio if you can tape a bass player, for instance, and use him to back a group like this—Giorgio can fade him out, bring him back in, at any level, just by touching a button. Having the man here for hours would waste his time and ours, and he might not get on with the group, might not be able to synchronise his free time with theirs. Anything can go wrong if everything's live.'

'Who are this group?' asked Vicky, watching the young men picking up their guitars and tuning them.

Giorgio told her an Italian name she'd never heard before.

'You wouldn't know them,' Ricco said. 'They're very popular here, but they don't play outside Italy yet.'

They were skinny young men with dark hair and eyes, all wearing T-shirts and faded blue jeans.

Giorgio depressed his mike key and said something. The boys in the studio looked up, waving, then caught sight of Vicky and at once whistled and grinned at her, shouting something.

She laughed, and Giorgio asked, 'You speak some Italian?'

She shook her head. 'I'm afraid I only know a few phrases yet, but I'm working on it.'

'They said you were very sexy,' Ricco told her with a cool intonation. 'And what are you doing tonight?'

'Oh,' she said, laughing again. That was what she had thought they said, but she didn't admit it.

'Tell them she isn't available,' Ricco told Giorgio with sardonic emphasis and a sideways glance at her. 'Tell them she's English and as cool as a cucumber sandwich.'

Giorgio grinned and talked into the mike. The musicians made caterwauling noises, waving their arms at Vicky in disgust.

'Okay, we try a recording now,' Giorgio said to Ricco.

Vicky loved the music; it was fast and modern with a good beat to it. One of the young men sang in Italian. She didn't understand the words but she picked up the feeling, her body swaying with the music. She began to notice when Giorgio was introducing some of his electronic wizardry, the rhythmic note of the bass, the drums, the echo. It was fascinating to see how the sound was mixed; the men working the electronic equipment had sensitive, quick-moving hands, and they operated their switches with as much skill as the young musicians in the studio.

When the group stopped playing Giorgio wound back the tape and played it for them. They sat on their stools, listening, faces intent.

Giorgio talked to them in Italian and they answered; Vicky didn't know what was being said. She looked at Ricco, who gave her a wry smile and translated.

'Giorgio thinks they weren't playing tightly enough. They weren't coming in on exactly the right beat at the right moment all together, as they should. The lead guitar is saying they'll be tighter next take.'

He kept his voice very low so as not to disturb Giorgio and his assistant. After a few minutes the group played again, and again Giorgio wound back the tape and played it for them before they had another of their earnest discussions.

Ricco glanced at his watch. 'I'm afraid we'll have to go,' he told her. 'I have an appointment at six and I can't miss it.'

He stood up and drew back her chair as she got to her feet. Giorgio took off his headphones, swivelling to smile and say goodbye.

'Drop in at the fish tank any time, as long as you give me notice you're coming.'

'The fish tank?' she asked, puzzled, and he nodded to the glass wall.

'That's what it looks like from down there in the studio—a big fish tank in the wall. That's what the boys call it.'

'Thank you very much for letting me eavesdrop, I enjoyed it enormously.'

'Good, nice to meet you. *Ciao*, Ricco.'

Giorgio was totally absorbed in his work again before they had left the room. Vicky looked back through the porthole and saw him with his headphones on, leaning forward to talk to the studio.

'*Did* you enjoy it?' Ricco asked as they made their way back to the Lamborghini. 'I know you told Giorgio you did, but you English are so polite. You don't always mean what you say—that's what gives your nation the reputation of being hypocrites.'

'I'm not a hypocrite,' Vicky retorted indignantly. 'And I meant what I said, it was really fascinating. I could have stayed there all day.'

'I'll try to make sure you have another chance to watch a session, then,' said Ricco, opening the car door for her to get in.

As they were driving back to the office a lorry backed out of a narrow alley, without warning, right into their path, and Ricco braked with such force that Vicky almost went through the windscreen.

Ricco yelled furious Italian at the lorry driver, who yelled back before driving off, making an insulting gesture through his window at them.

'Are you okay?' Ricco asked, turning to look anxiously at her.

'I think so.' She had been shocked more than hurt.

He leaned over and kissed her lightly. 'You're shaking! Thank heavens you had your seatbelt on.'

She couldn't think of anything to say; his gentle kiss had undermined her again. Had what happened with Miller and Sunny made her too cynical, too suspicious? Was she wrong about Ricco? She felt confused and disturbed as they drove on—she wished she knew for certain what sort of man he was, and at the same time she had a sinking feeling that it was too late to find out. She watched his profile secretly, brooding over him.

She had been too sure of herself when she met Miller. She had thought she knew her feelings, she had been ready to leap into love without knowing Miller at all. This time she had been determined not to let Ricco get to her. At least she had known the dangers, she hadn't just charged straight ahead into disaster, but her wariness hadn't saved her. She had known on Saturday night that it was a little more than physical attraction between herself and Ricco. Her emotions were involved again, and she had a premonition that she was going to wish she had never met him.

I don't want to fall in love again, she thought grimly. Or is that the wrong tense? Am I in love already? What else explains the odd effect he has on me every time I see him? The frayed temper, the crazy excitement, the sudden happiness and a moment later the stupid misery? Being in love was like a spring day—sunshine one minute, showers the next, and an awareness of being alive that was sharper than at any other time.

She didn't want to be in love; it hurt too much. She might be called a coward, but she wasn't going to be called a fool again.

When she and Ricco walked into the art department they found Andrea standing in front of a line of advertising posters which he had pinned up on the wall. He looked round, grimacing at them.

'Look at these—would you believe it? They printed the wrong colours, transposed the yellow and purple—look!'

Vicky and Ricco looked, faces blank.

'They look fine to me,' said Ricco.

'I like them,' Vicky agreed.

'I didn't say they weren't okay, I said the colours had been switched,' Andrea grunted impatiently. 'As it happens, it works, but I want you to talk to those crazy printers, Ricco. Kick them around, get it home that if they do this again we'll take our work elsewhere.'

'The artwork is really stunning, isn't it?' Vicky

said, sighing. Whoever had done the poster had
been a genius. It was spectacular—a wild crash of
colours which immediately made itself noticed.

Andrea shrugged. 'It's passable.'

They began to talk about the artwork while Ricco
perched on the side of a desk and listened, his face
amused. It must have been half an hour later that
the door opened and Bianca swept into the room in
one of her lush minks, her ears glittering with
diamonds in a swinging cascade.

'*Ciao, caro,*' she said to Ricco, kissing him and
purring like a cat in that long white throat.

Vicky watched, her teeth tight with jealousy. She
hadn't liked Bianca on sight, but she hated her at
that moment, watching the other woman curve an
arm round Ricco's neck, gazing up into his eyes.

'What are you doing here, Bianca?' Ricco asked,
smiling.

Bianca spun, her diamond earrings flashing. She
threw Vicky a malicious smile and Vicky tensed in
alarm. Had Bianca recognised her on the cover of
that magazine? Why was she staring like that, an
odd smile curving her red mouth?

'I bring a surprise for *her,*' Bianca said in thickly
accented English.

She walked to the door and opened it, and Vicky
went white as she saw Miller in the doorway.

# CHAPTER TEN

VICKY'S feet seemed to be rooted to the spot. She had had nightmares about this happening and woken up to find that they had been just that—a nightmare. This wasn't something she would wake up from; this was real, it was happening.

'Vicky!' Miller was acting—that much she took in at a glance. He would have done well in silent films, he had a real talent for sweeping mime. He came towards her with outstretched arms, radiating bittersweet reproach, love, forgiveness.

Vicky felt like kicking him in the shins.

Andrea was chewing his pencil. 'He looks like someone. Who is it? I know that face, I never forget a face.' He opened his mouth, his jaw dropped and so did the pencil. It rolled across the floor. Andrea exclaimed with bated breath: 'My God! It's Miller Osborne. I'd swear he's Miller Osborne—or his double. Ricco, isn't he Miller Osborne?'

'What the hell is going on?' demanded Ricco in a voice that almost made the windows shake.

Bianca told him in cooing Italian. Vicky was rather glad suddenly that she hadn't yet learnt enough of the language to know what Bianca was saying about her. Whatever it was, it made Ricco look as if he could eat nails.

Miller tried to kiss Vicky. She jerked her head away and all he kissed was her cheek.

'How could you do it? I nearly went out of my mind with worry, I thought you'd been kidnapped,' said Miller.

Over his shoulder Vicky saw Sunny and her stomach clenched. Just the sight of him made her feel sick. He had a pack of photographers with him, they must have been waiting outside to give Miller time to get her in his arms. Miller smiled down at her as if he hadn't noticed she was as stiff as a jointed wooden doll in his embrace. He swung her deftly so that the photographers would snap his best side. It wasn't just that he was acting; he had a script to work to, and it was obvious who had written it—Sunny, the master of the set-up, the magician of the publicity release. Miller even had his moves chalked out for him.

'Get out of my office!' snarled Ricco, leaping between them and the photographers just as the flashbulbs went off.

'Hey, what do you think you're doing, mister?' Miller complained, scowling at him. 'Get out of the way—you ruined the picture! Sorry about that, guys—we'll do it again. Hey, Sunny, get this jerk out of here, will you?'

That was when Ricco hit him. Miller went down like a tree, mowing Sunny down on the way. The photographers got their picture and Miller's best side was camera forward. Vicky didn't care how she looked, or whether she was in the picture at all. She was staring at Ricco and he was staring back as if he meant to hit her next. She had never seen him look so angry.

'Is it true?' he asked through his teeth.

Miller was scrambling foggily to his knees, holding his jaw and making an incredulous noise. It was the stunt man who did all that stuff in his pictures, not the star. Getting a punch on the jaw was not written into his contract. His insurance company weren't going to like this.

'Sunny!' he yelled.

'Answer me,' Ricco told Vicky, his hands screwed into fists at his side. 'Were you going to marry him?'

'I . . .' Vicky couldn't get the words out. She had a form of emotional lockjaw; everything inside her had frozen. So she ran. It had become a habit, perhaps. Running was the easiest way out and at that moment the wisest, because the longer she stayed around the more pictures the photographers were going to get.

Miller had forgotten her; he was picking Sunny up from the floor and anxiously dusting him down. He couldn't operate without Sunny there to feed him his lines, tell him what to do and think. Vicky still found Sunny terrifying, but she wasn't running away from him this time—she was running away from Ricco. The look in his blue eyes had made her knees give. He hated her. She felt so miserable as she saw that look on his face that she couldn't bear to see it any more.

She hadn't quite got away yet, though. She heard the following feet, the shouted questions, the pleas for her to stop. The reporters like bloodhounds poured down the stairs, shoving each other in their attempts to be the first to reach her. Vicky ran through the front door of the building with the pack on her heels, thinking wildly: How am I to get away from them? She had no car, there were no buses around here. She simply put on more speed, and saw ahead of her on a corner a lady in a large blue picture hat getting out of a taxi. Vicky put on another spurt, breathless by now, her chest heaving.

A man was running from the opposite direction towards the taxi, his hand held up. Vicky pushed past the lady in the picture hat, who was just paying the driver, and threw herself into the back of the taxi.

'*Signore, per favore, rapidemente! La stazione!*'

'*Centrale?*' he asked, tucking the money his last fare had given him into a wallet.

'*Si, si, grazie.*'

They moved off a second or two before the pack caught up with them. Vicky peered back and saw them engulfing the lady in the picture hat and the man who had run to catch the taxi, too. She saw the reporters talking to them. Demanding where she had asked to be taken?

Vicky bit her lip, wondering what to do. Go to Susan's house? But the reporters might find out about her cousin from Bianca and descend on the house in droves, giving poor Susan the scare of her life.

She dared not go back to Ricco's villa, that was too obvious, and anyway, she was in no hurry to face Ricco either. Where could she go? Suddenly she had a brainwave and leaned forward.

'*Signore?*'

'*Si?*'

She told him to take her to Andrea's house. Nobody would think of looking for her there; she would have a breathing space in which to think and work out what to do next, and she wouldn't be giving Susan any trouble. Vicky knew how much her cousin would hate having a herd of reporters trampling through the garden, shouting through the letterbox, peering in at the windows.

The first thing she must do when she reached

Andrea's was ask if she could use the phone. She must ring Susan and warn her.

Lucy opened the door, her expression taken aback. 'Oh, hallo.' She noted Vicky's flushed and dishevelled state, frowning. 'Is something wrong?'

'Lucy, can I come in? I need your help, I'm sorry to be a nuisance, but I'm in bad trouble.'

Lucy wordlessly waved her into the house and Vicky collapsed into a chair, her mind in a state of utter disarray. Lucy looked hard at her.

'You need a cup of tea.'

Vicky laughed, well-nigh hysterical by then. Lucy paused on her way to the kitchen.

'On second thoughts, we'll make that a stiff brandy.'

'I'm sorry to be a . . .'

'Don't say it again, you're not a nuisance,' Lucy produced a bottle of brandy, uncorked it, held it over a glass. 'Say when.'

'Oh, please, that's more than enough,' Vicky said breathlessly. Her eye fell on the telephone on a table near the window. 'Lucy, may I use your phone? It's urgent.'

'Be my guest.' Lucy poured herself a brandy too. 'Am I going to need this? Yes, I think so,' she said, sipping. 'Oh . . . Andrea is okay, isn't he?'

Vicky was lifting the phone. 'What? Oh, yes, yes, he's fine. I was just with him in the office, but . . .' She swallowed and stopped talking until she had got Susan on the phone. 'Susan, listen, it's me, Vicky— no, don't panic. Listen, just listen—Miller is here. Yes, in Florence. No, don't scream! I've got away from them and I'm quite safe, but the press may come to your place. Look, get David on the phone, tell him what's happened, then drive to his office and stay with him at all costs. Don't go back home until you've checked that the press aren't around.' She listened to Susan's aghast exclamations. 'I'm sorry, Susan, very sorry to have dropped all this on you. No, I wouldn't just stay put if I were you, because I know those people, they'll camp out all round the house if they think you're in there, and they'll keep on ringing the bell and trying to get in until doomsday.'

When she put the phone down Lucy was sitting staring at her, her brandy glass already empty. 'I think,' said Lucy, 'I'm going to need another brandy. A bigger one this time.'

Vicky came back towards her and sat down, nursing her brandy glass. 'I owe you an explanation.'

'Let me make myself comfortable—I get the feeling this is going to take a while.' Lucy curled up in her chair like a child about to hear a bedtime story. 'Right, fire away—no, wait—do you want some more of this?' She gestured to the brandy bottle.

Vicky shook her head and plunged into her explanation. Lucy didn't interrupt once, listening with fascination while she sipped her second glass of brandy.

Only when Vicky stopped talking did Lucy comment. 'I must say, it's better than *Dallas*. I wish I'd been there. You say Ricco hit Miller Obsborne? Miller Osborne—good heavens, it's amazing just to talk to someone who actually knows him!' Her eyes skated over Vicky in her powder-blue top and white pleated skirt. 'And you were engaged to him! I don't know how you could walk out on a man like Miller Osborne. He's so gorgeous!'

Vicky smiled weakly. 'Well, you know the saying
. . . one woman's man is another woman's poison.'

Lucy laughed. 'I suppose he can't be as terrific as
he seems in his films, he wouldn't be human if he
was. All I can say is you must have great strength of
character. I'd guess that a lot of women would put
up with the odd flaw in him simply for all that lovely
money—he must be terrifically rich. He's been
making films for years, hasn't he? Is he forty or so?'

'Oh, no, he's only in his thirties.'

'He seems to have been around much longer than
that.'

'He was a hit in his first film, and his career has
been very well stage-managed.'

'By this agent of his?'

'Sunny—yes, I think he was the master-mind.' It
certainly hadn't been Miller. He was no fool, but he
was more concerned with how he looked in films
than in choosing the right parts. It had undoubtedly
been Sunny who made the clever decisions. Was
that why Miller relied implicitly on him? Probably.

Lucy watched her curiously. 'Is *he* still in love
with *you*? I read about all this, a week ago, in the
last pop paper I saw from England. My old mum
sends a batch to me every month, to keep me in
touch with home news. I don't know why I didn't
recognise you, there was a big picture of you in the
paper, but it didn't ring any bells—well, I'd never
met you then, so it wouldn't, and when we did meet
I suppose I didn't connect you with the missing
Vicky . . .' she paused, knitted her forehead. 'See? I
can't even remember your surname.'

'Gavin.'

'Oh, yes. Gavin. Vicky's not that unusual, of
course, and anyway, Andrea had been talking about

you for a couple of weeks and calling you Ricco's girl-friend, so . . .'

'What?' Vicky sat up, very flushed. 'Calling me what?'

'Well, Andrea has a simple mind,' Lucy said apologetically, 'Ricco talked him into taking you on, and Andrea just leapt to the obvious conclusion—obvious for a man, that is,' She grinned, but Vicky wasn't laughing.

'Well, please tell your husband that I'm not Ricco's girlfriend.' Vicky was very much on her dignity.

'Even if Ricco did knock your ex-fiancé down,' Lucy supplied drily, and Vicky's flush deepened.

'Miller called him a jerk, that's why he did that.'

'Yes, I can see that that would get under Ricco's skin. And he has got a hot temper at times, although he can be a positive lamb,' Lucy smiled at Vicky. 'So what are you going to do now? You can't keep hiding, you know. Sooner or later you're going to have to face Miller and talk it out with him.'

'Not with the press for an audience,' Vicky got up and prowled impatiently round the room like a caged tiger. 'That's why I went away without seeing him, I knew Sunny would pull a trick like this on me. Miller can't even sneeze without the media there to commemorate it. If I had married Miller, I might have found myself going on honeymoon with TV cameras and a busload of pressmen for company. And I began to think Miller himself might not show up.' She swallowed, grimacing. 'Just Sunny.'

Lucy's face grew grave. 'I see why you felt you had to get away. What's he like, this Sunny?'

'Loathsome.'

'That bad?'

'Worse. I'm being polite about him.'

Lucy laughed, then shook her head. 'It isn't funny, is it?'

'No. I'm scared of snakes too, but if I had a choice between being shut up in a room full of snakes or a room with Sunny, I'd try to learn to like snakes,' Vicky looked down at her bare forearms. 'Look, goose-pimples, at the mere idea of it. He makes my skin crawl.'

'Are you sure it wasn't because of him you left Miller—rather than because you fell out of love with Miller himself?'

'I'm certain. It was a mixture of both. Miller knew, you see; he knew Sunny had made a pass at me, I told him, and he didn't care. He laughed; he thought I was naïve for being so shocked. Sunny told me Miller and he often shared girls.'

'Shared them?' Lucy looked shocked now. 'Do you mean . . . shared them?'

'That's what I mean,' Vicky nodded, and Lucy took a deep breath.

'I think you were right to run away. What an awful let down, and I thought Miller Osborne seemed so genuine.' The phone rang, and Lucy went towards it at once.

'If it's Ricco, don't tell him I'm here!' Vicky burst out, stiffening.

'I won't,' Lucy picked up the phone and asked warily: 'Hallo?' Her face relaxed. 'Oh, hello, darling.' She looked at Vicky, smiling. 'Don't worry, it's Andrea.' Then into the phone she said: 'Yes, she's here—how did you guess?' then listened, smiling. 'Very shrewd of you. She thought she'd better not go back to the villa or her cousin's place in case the press turned up there. Yes, that's right. Her cousin knows, yes. She's gone to meet her husband, they're staying clear until the press leave,'

'Ask him not to tell Ricco,' whispered Vicky.

'Vicky doesn't want you to tell Ricco, Andrea,' Lucy said. 'She seems scared of what he may do—were you there when he hit Miller Osborne ... really? No? I didn't hear that. What, all the way down the stairs? Was he hurt? From what Vicky has just been telling me, he deserved it.' She listened without speaking for a few minutes, then said: 'I'll see you later, then, darling. Goodbye.'

She hung up and looked round at Vicky. 'Ricco ran that agent out of the building after you'd gone, got hold of his jacket and threw him out bodily. Andrea says he threw him down the stairs but as he got up and walked off after that he can't have been hurt. Andrea was probably exaggerating. He seems to have enjoyed the whole thing.'

Vicky closed her eyes. 'Did the photographers get a picture of that, too?'

'Andrea didn't say. I hope so, I'd love to see it.' Lucy looked at her watch. 'Look, I'm starving after all this mad excitement, aren't you? Why don't I make some lunch? You stay here, have a rest—nobody will disturb you, the children are at school. I'll call you when lunch is ready.'

'You're being very kind, thank you, Lucy.' Vicky felt a strong tendency to cry, which was silly, but it had been a very emotional morning, and Lucy's kindness on top of all that seemed just too much.

'Nothing of the sort. I haven't had so much fun for ages; you've brought a splash of mad colour into my humdrum life.' Lucy gave her a smile and went out, closing the door. Vicky curled up in her chair, her head drooping sideways, and stared at the clock.

It had been two hours since she ran like a hunted hare from Ricco's office. Just two hours. It felt like a hundred years. What was she to do now? She couldn't ever go back there, people would stare. Ricco must hate her.

She had lied to him over and over again. He wouldn't forgive her for that. She closed her eyes, tears stinging under her lids. She hadn't meant to care, but somehow it had happened—she must be very weak-willed. She had known on Saturday that it was more than just a passing attraction she felt for Ricco. There had been intense passion between them, in the dark, with the storm raging outside, lightning showing them each other's faces. Perhaps that was how love always happened—you saw the other darkly, by brief flashes of illumination. That was how it had been with Miller, too, and when she saw him clearly she knew it was all illusion.

She was afraid it would be that way with Ricco. What did she know about him after all? She hadn't even met him much more than a month ago. She might know him a little better than she had got to know Miller before their engagement, but perhaps she was wrong about him too, perhaps he wasn't the man she thought he was, and she didn't think she could bear another crass mistake. When love goes wrong, nothing goes right—wasn't that a song title? It was spot on anyway, she had learnt that.

Suddenly she heard Lucy's voice rising outside. Lucy was almost shouting. Vicky sat up, rigid with shock.

'You can't see her! I promised her—please listen, I promised her I wouldn't let anybody in, she doesn't want to see you.'

It was Miller, Vicky thought, getting up and backing from the door. If she could have seen anywhere to hide she would have leapt into it. Lucy wasn't going to let him in here—was she? But Miller and Sunny might force their way past her, they weren't above that, and Lucy would be no match for both of them.

'But I promised her,' Lucy protested, very close to the door. Vicky knew that Lucy was trying to warn her, give her time to . . . to what?

She looked round the room. Where could she go? The window was the only exit, of course. She crept over to it and slid it up very carefully, making as little sound as possible. The window looked out into a narrow alley, and there was quite a short drop to the ground. Vicky climbed on to the sill and slid her legs through, but she was too late. She heard a movement behind her, looked upwards, backwards, expecting to see Miller or Sunny, but it was Ricco and he was striding towards her, his eyes hard and menacing.

'Oh, no, you don't!'

He caught hold of her waist and pulled. Vicky struggled to throw herself forward, outward. Her feet sank. Ricco dragged them upwards again. A small boy in a pair of red shorts stood with his thumb in his mouth, watching, in the centre of the alley.

Inch by wriggling inch, Vicky was drawn back into the room, feeling like an escaping worm hauled back to the surface by a much stronger bird. From upside down Ricco's nose did look rather like a beak, and there was no doubt about it, his feathers were distinctly ruffled. She made a last attempt, calling to the boy outside: 'Help!' Her last hope just stared, bolt-eyed.

Ricco dragged her into the room and dropped her unceremoniously on the floor while he shut the window. By the time he had turned round Vicky was on her feet again, slightly breathless, staggering a little, but making for the door as fast as she could.

Ricco got between her and her exit somehow. One minute she was within arms' reach of escape, the next she was slamming into Ricco's very solid body.

'Now!' he said, and she resisted a crazy temptation to lean on him and give up. His deep chest looked so comfortingly firm.

'Don't you threaten me!' she defied, her head going back so that she could glare at him.

'Oh, I haven't even started yet! I knew—right from the day we first met—that there was something you were running from. I even knew, thought I knew, what it was—it had to be a man.'

'Why,' she asked scornfully, 'had it to be a man? It could have been anything! But whatever the question, the answer is *always* "a man", isn't it? I could have been running away from anything, a job, the police, a blackmailer—why did you have to leap to the conclusion that it was a man?'

'It was, though, wasn't it?' he demanded unanswerably, and she clenched her teeth and didn't answer. Ricco steered her backwards as though they were dancing a strange new ballroom dance, pushed her down on the couch and sat next to her, an arm across her barring escape.

'I've talked to Susan,' he said conversationally.

Vicky looked at him sharply. 'I told her to . . .'

'Go to David? She did. I went to David too, and

found her there. They wouldn't tell me where you were, but they told me a great deal about Miller Osborne and that creep he comes with—I was glad I'd thrown him out on his ear after I'd listened to what Susan had to say about him.'

Vicky couldn't help a weakening towards him, remembering that he had flung Sunny down the narrow stairs at the office.

'I was glad, too. Thank you.'

'You're welcome,' he said formally. 'Why didn't you tell me what you were scared of? Why lie to me? Didn't you trust me?'

She looked up quickly, biting her lip. 'Yes, of course!' But she hadn't, had she? She had thought he was another Miller and had been very wary of him. His blue eyes watched her with comprehension and anger.

'Stop it now, Vicky. No more lies. You didn't trust me, did you?'

'I didn't trust anybody, except Susan and David,' she admitted huskily.

'There was no married boss who chased you and wanted to have an affair with you?'

She shook her head, looking down.

'Your name's Vicky Gavin, not Vicky Lloyd.'

She nodded.

'But your parents are dead and Susan is your cousin?'

'Yes, all that was true, and everything I told you about college and my job—it was Sunny who got me fired.'

'I know, Susan told me.'

She looked up, mouth wry. 'She talked a lot, for Susan! She's usually so shy with you.'

'She was worried about you.' I had to persuade

her to talk to me at all, it wasn't easy.' His hand shot out and caught her chin, forced her face round towards him, his blue eyes very dark and intent, insisting that she meet their gaze.

'Did you love him?' he asked, his voice rough.

'Did Susan tell you how I met Miller?'

He shook his head, so she explained that first meeting, the beauty of the still autumn morning, Miller on a big black horse, London still waking up beyond the gold and crimson trees.

'High romance,' Ricco said tersely.

'He's a film actor, he knows how to set up scenes, how to manipulate the emotions. It's second nature to him, just as it's second nature to make sure a camera always finds him with his best profile ready,'

'You still haven't answered my question! Did you love him in the beginning?'

'I was trying to answer it. I loved the whole story line—that was what I fell for—the girl walking in a park, the handsome stranger on a black stallion. The stuff of fairy tales, how could I resist it? We got engaged almost overnight, and then I woke up! I found that my fairy prince was a weak, conceited man with very few morals, and that the wicked wizard was his best friend and had him right under his thumb. It wasn't even a wicked spell, because Miller didn't want to break it. He thought Sunny was terrific, he relied on him. He'd have handed me over to him without a second thought.'

Ricco clenched his teeth, going pale. She saw him swallow. 'So that part of it was true, too? That animal did make a pass at you?'

'Sunny's corrupt. He always had Miller's women when Miller tired of them.'

Ricco put his arms round her and cradled her like a baby. 'I'll kill him for you,' he said hoarsely. 'What did he do to you?'

She closed her eyes and let her body yield. His warmth crept into her, encircled her, made her feel safe.

'I didn't give him the chance. As soon as I saw what was in his mind, I just ran away and came here.'

'Bastard,' muttered Ricco. He made it sound very Latin. 'I wish I'd hit him a damned sight harder.'

'Oh, forget him, forget both of them,' Vicky said. 'That's what I'm going to do. They don't matter.'

Ricco kissed her temples, his mouth slid down over her short blonde hair, pressed softly into her throat.

'My hair's dyed, you know,' Vicky said a little anxiously. He had to know it all now, the whole truth and nothing but the truth—but she was afraid he might be disappointed when he realised she wasn't a real blonde. Italians liked fair women, didn't they?

'Of course I knew,' Ricco said, his lips just under her chin now and the sound of his voice vibrating through her bone structure. 'Do you think I'm stupid? Think I can't tell a genuine blonde from a dyed one?'

'I'm really brunette.' His hands had crept about like little mice, she kept finding them in unexpected places and they made shivers run up and down her spine. She dislodged one which had made a nest between her breasts. 'Lucy may come in.'

'Not until I call her,' said Ricco with typically splendid assurance. 'Why were you climbing out of the window?'

'I thought you would be angry.'

'I am angry! You should have confided in me, trusted me. I'm more than angry—I'm hurt.'

'I'm sorry,' she said, genuinely contrite, looking up at him anxiously.

'So I should think! You have a lot to make up to me for.' He looked at her mouth, his lips parted, breathing raggedly. 'Vicky, darling,' he whispered, and she lifted her mouth with an eagerness which might shame her later but over which at that moment she had no control. She needed to have him kiss her, she needed it badly.

Their lips met, and a rush of sudden, burning passion swept through her. She stopped thinking, her arms going round his neck and clinging, her body limp and yielding in his arms. She had been trying to fight the way she felt about him from the first day they met because she was afraid that she was going to make the same mistake again, fool herself that a physical attraction was real love. The attraction between herself and Ricco had flashed at once, like summer lightning, like the sudden storm that had blown up on Saturday in the heat of the night, but she had not dared to believe in it. It had been too much of a risk, and she had been afraid of burning her fingers again.

She had known the other night, though, known deep inside herself that the way she felt about Ricco was nothing like the infatuation she had had for Miller. That had worn off almost at once, although she still hadn't got to know Miller very well—he was never there, he didn't give her a chance to discover what sort of man there really was under the beautiful mask. Vicky had a sneaking suspicion that Miller did not dare let anyone too close in case they found out just what sort of man he really was, but she had found out and she had despised him.

She knew far more about Ricco, she liked him as well as being fiercely attracted by him. She knew she could work with him, live with him, share the future with him. In the end that was what love was all about—sharing life together.

Much later, Ricco said grimly: 'If we have any more trouble from Osborne and his manager, leave them to me. I'll welcome the chance to tell them a few home truths.'

'It was Bianca who told them where to find me, wasn't it?' Vicky said, lowering her lashes and watching him through them.

'She recognised some picture of you and rang Osborne to tell him you were in Florence,' said Ricco, his eyes hard.

'She doesn't like me,' Vicky said, fighting down the jealousy she still felt. Ricco had said he loved her a moment ago, she wasn't going to doubt it, yet she couldn't help remembering that night she saw him on the loggia with Bianca. They knew each other so well.

'She hates your guts,' agreed Ricco, his mouth quizzical.

Their eyes met and he smiled at her expression. 'She's in love with you,' Vicky said tartly.

'Bianca? She's another narcissistic creature, like Osborne—they don't have normal human feelings. They're in love with their own image.' Ricco played with her hair, his eyes wry. 'Bianca is possessive, too. She didn't like it when she guessed I was in love with you.' He watched her with glinting amusement. 'It meant I wouldn't pay her so much attention in future. She's not in love with me, but she likes to have me dancing to her tune.'

'Did you? Dance to her tune?' Vicky asked jealously.

'It was business, Vicky, purely business. I have a couple of dozen such demanding stars on my books. When they're in Florence they think I belong to them.' He smiled at her passionately. 'But now I belong to you.' She closed her eyes, weak and breathing dangerously fast. She heard the deep sea swell of her racing blood in her ears and muttered shakily: 'I think I've got high blood pressure.'

'I've had it ever since I saw you at the airport that first day,' Ricco said drily. 'So very English—nose in the air, cool as a cucumber sandwich, just asking to get kissed or slapped or both.'

'Do I get a choice?'

'You get me,' he told her. 'That will have to be enough for you.'

Vicky's arms tightened round his neck. He was enough for her; she had a feeling he would always be enough.

# New This spring

# *Harlequin Category Romance Specials!*

## New Mix

## 4 Regencies—for more wit, tradition, etiquette . . . and romance

## 2 Gothics—for more suspense, drama, adventure . . . and romance

### Regencies

***A Hint of Scandal*** by Alberta Sinclair
She was forced to accept his offer of marriage, but could she live with her decision?

***The Primrose Path*** by Jean Reece
She was determined to ruin his reputation and came close to destroying her own!

***Dame Fortune's Fancy*** by Phyllis Taylor Pianka
She knew her dream of love could not survive the barrier of his family tradition. . . .

***The Winter Picnic*** by Dixie McKeone
All the signs indicated they were a mismatched couple, yet she could not ignore her heart's request. . . .

### Gothics

***Mirage on the Amazon*** by Mary Kistler
Her sense of foreboding did not prepare her for what lay in waiting at journey's end. . . .

***Island of Mystery*** by Margaret M. Scariano
It was the perfect summer job, or so she thought—until it became a nightmare of danger and intrigue.

### Don't miss any of them!

BPA-CAT/87-1

# PATRICIA MATTHEWS

America's First Lady of Romance upholds her long
standing reputation as a bestselling romance novelist
with . . .

*Enchanted*

Caught in the steamy heat of America's New South,
Rebecca Trenton finds herself torn between two
brothers—she yearns for one but a dark secret binds
her to the other.

# Take
# 4 novels
# and a
# surprise gift
# FREE

# Harlequin Presents

## Coming Next Month

Available in May wherever paperback books are sold, or through
Harlequin Reader Service:

In the U.S.
901 Fuhrmann Blvd.
P.O. Box 1397
Buffalo, N.Y. 14240-1397

In Canada
P.O. Box 603
Fort Erie, Ontario
L2A 5X3